The Mirror

H. R. Kasper

Enjoy!!

H. R. Kasper

THE MIRROR

For Brennen—both Leigh and I would tell a very different tale without you. Milliaria nequit separari.

THE MIRROR

THE MIRROR

CONTENTS

THE MIRROR

ACKNOWLEDGMENTS

First, to my family—my sister, my dad, mom, and grandma—thanks for all the support, the helpful comments and suggestions and for the investment you showed in the story. My friends, Grace, Allisa, and Olivia, the enthusiasm you showed has spurred me on through all three parts of this book. Thank you to my teammates Anna Rose and Alaina—your patience in waiting for the #nextchapter has always been impressive! Brennen, my best friend…thanks for the advice when I wanted it, the constructive criticism when I deserved it, and the encouragement when I needed it. You shaped this story in so many ways that I have yet to discover them all. Thank you. Lastly, to a God who is good…all the time, no matter what.

Part I: Vitreusia's Hero

"Come, Leigh, come with me…"

THE MIRROR

I.

I found myself looking into it constantly as I packed the endless boxes. Gazing not at myself, but at the window in my bedroom, the knick knacks on my dresser. Everything looked different in that rectangular mirror with a golden metal border.

When I was younger, I used to wonder if I could step through that mirror and find a fantastical fairy-tale world on the other side. Throughout the years, when my life became suddenly or unusually stressful, I would start to look pensively at the mirror, wishing I could step through it like in my childhood fantasies and find something wonderful on the other side.

Lately, the events happening all around me had been the very definition of stressful. Over the course of the past week, I'd been betrayed and backstabbed by my (supposedly) best friend, found out I was leaving the seaside home and city I loved, and somehow racked up enough tardy notes to get detention for a week. Had my parents not pleaded with the principal and the administrator, I might've been expelled.

I forced myself to stop thinking about the troubles at school, but when those left my mind, the fact that I was moving to Missouri entered. I bit my lip. That thought wouldn't cheer me up any.

I turned my gaze towards the mirror, running my eyes over its golden borders, finding some sort of odd comfort in the simple act of gazing at it. I ignored my reflection, my tall, willowy form, my deep blue eyes framed by straight, jet-black hair. Adrienne's harsh voice came roaring into my head, a flashback to the recent past. *I'm not your friend, let alone your best friend.* I could still see that condescending smile, feel that stab of betrayal ripping through my heart. I heard my dad, saying to me as he, my mom, and I ate dinner, "I've been relocated." Lastly, I saw the cold look of the principal, staring me down as I shifted uncomfortably in the bad-high-schooler chair.

I swallowed hard, a tear forming in the corner of my eye. Without even knowing what I was doing, I reached out towards the mirror, to touch it with my hand. A voice inside me asked, "Leigh Kaitlyn Kline, have you lost your mind completely? It's just a mirror. You know that in two seconds your fingers will touch cold, hard glass." But in spite of that, I kept reaching for that world I knew did not exist, a world where dreams came true and only the bad guys got stabbed in the back. As the 'voice' had predicted, seconds later my fingertips pressed against the glass I had so hoped wasn't there.

With a sigh, I pressed my hand on the mirror. Suddenly, the reflection of my hot pink bedroom was gone. It dissolved like an ice cube in hot water, and left behind a black void. I froze, hardly daring to breathe.

Moments later I heard a sweet, silky voice. "Leigh, dear, I have waited for this moment for a very long time. Come, Leigh, come with me. You will never feel the pang of sadness again." I took a deep breath, considering the decision for a split second. I stepped through the golden doorway, into the thin, cold darkness, and watched everything that was familiar slowly but surely fade away, the velvety blackness enveloping every part of me. I hovered there in the nothingness for what seemed like forever. I stayed where I was, puzzled. Suddenly my heart skipped a beat. There was a hand on my shoulder.

I turned to face one of the most beautiful creatures I had ever seen in my life. I call her a creature because, although she certainly looked human, she was so stunning that she seemed immortal. Delicate, wispy light green curls framed her round, porcelain face, which was dotted here and there with freckles. Her eyes were a deep, dark purple that reminded me of concentrated grape juice, and a light emitted from her, a golden yellow glow. She smiled, her teeth whiter than the first snowfall. "You have made it, Leigh." I knit my dark eyebrows together. What was she talking about? "Made it to where?" I asked.

"Vitreusia," she replied, "The land of reflections. Come, follow me," she said, sweetly but firmly as she held out a thin, delicate hand. "My name is Christina." Although my parents, had, indeed, given me 'the stranger talk', I felt deep within that Christina would never hurt me. I nodded and took her hand into mine, and together we walked through the void.

By this time my mind was overflowing with questions, so I chose the one that I thought would shed the most light on what was going on and spoke up. "Are there other people here?"

"Human beings?" asked Christina, wading through the empty darkness.

"Yes."

"Many like you have found their way here," she answered, sounding a little preoccupied. Hmm. She hadn't given me much to go on.

Suddenly she stopped short and chanted something in a foreign language, holding fast to my hand. A crack of light began to show through the blackness, and I drew in a sharp breath at the sight that met my eyes.

It would have been a beautiful town, had it not been in utter chaos and turmoil. Of the twenty houses that I counted, about ten were on fire, the flames licking at their structures. Cries for help and screams of terror filled the air. Christina stood where she was, her dark eyes glimmering with oncoming tears. "This is not the Vitreusia I left," she said in her silky whisper. "Something has gone horribly wrong. Stay here, Leigh. I must help my people." and she dashed off towards the tiny city.

"Wait!" I called after her. "What if.." but she was already far away. "You don't...come..back.."

I kept an eye on her green head as long as I could, and then I saw her slight figure vanish into one of the flaming buildings. "Oh, no," I said under my breath. My heart beat faster as the minutes ticked by and I did not see her emerge. "Come on, Christina, where are you?" I mumbled to myself, fidgeting with the golden chain of the locket that hung around my neck. More agonizing minutes passed with no sign of her.

I made a decision right then and there. I couldn't obey orders now, not when Christina's life was in danger. In those few minutes, I had begun to like her, and besides, what if the rest of the people in— Vitreusia—weren't as friendly?

Taking a deep breath, I hurried down to the village and ran towards the building Christina had gone into almost ten minutes ago.

I entered the flaming structure and started coughing from the smoke. My asthma was not going to help this situation one bit. "Christina?" I choked out, coughing like crazy. "Christina!" There was no response. I tore through the scorching building, my chest filling with burning pain, shouting, "Christina!! Christina!!"

I came to a door that had small flames coming up from the bottom. I tried to open it, but it did not budge. Desperately I threw my five foot seven inch frame against it once, twice, four times. The fourth time I rammed it the door fell down into the room, where a familiar form lay motionless on the floor, the flames creeping closer and closer. *Christina.*

I dashed to her side and felt her wrist. She had a pulse, albeit a very faint one. After further examination I discovered a large lump on her forehead.

Something must have fallen from above, knocking her out. But what? And why had she dashed into this flaming building in the first place? I had no time to ponder over those questions now. I had to get both of us out of the blazing structure. I looked around. There was only one way out, and that was through the doorway I'd broken down not five minutes ago. I chafed Christina's wrists, pleading, "Christina! Wake up! We have to get out of here! CHRISTINA!" But she remained unconscious. The smoke was really getting to me now, and the flames continued to lick across the wooden floors. Panic began to set in, and suddenly I heard a deafening *crash!*

A flaming board fell from the ceiling, right in front of the doorway, setting the woodwork ablaze. We were trapped! I attempted again, more earnestly now, to awaken Christina. In spite of my desperate, choking pleas, she laid there in my arms, oblivious to all around her. Closer and closer crept the flames. I was coughing uncontrollably, and I realized that soon I would pass out right next to Christina. I wondered what would happen if I died in Vitreusia..would everyone back in the real world never see me again? Would I wake up on the floor of my bedroom? It seemed that the answer to that question was short in coming. I gasped for air, but I couldn't get enough...the smoke was taking its toll. *"There has to be a way out of this!"* I thought. *"There has to be!"* Suddenly, I felt a burning sensation, and my body began to glow. This was it. So much for a better life.

II.

I braced myself for a terrible death..but nothing ever happened. I stopped coughing from the smoke—but the burning feeling remained, making my entire body feel like it was on fire. I opened my eyes and looked down at my hand. It was glowing, emitting a warm, yellowish light. *What was going on?*

I got off the floor, feeling oddly strong. Before I knew what I was doing, I picked Christina up, and held her in a fireman's carry. I looked for a way out, but saw none besides the blazing doorway I had come through nearly ten minutes ago. I decided to put my newfound superhuman strength to the test, and threw my shoulder against one of the walls. The whole structure shook and shimmied, but the wall stood firm. Again I threw myself against it, and we went through, the rest of the building collapsing as we fell onto the soft, springy turf. We were safe—for the time being, at least. Christina was still unconscious. I shook her violently, and her eyes fluttered open. She looked at me first with confusion, then anger, then admiration and awe. "What is it?" I asked, puzzled by what I saw in her deep, dark purple eyes.

"Leigh…" she said in her velvety voice, "you are the one!" She lost consciousness again. I sat there, confused—and then perceived a young man running over.

He was tall and lean, having azure hair and green eyes. A glow hung about him that was similar to Christina's. As he approached Christina and I, he looked at me curiously, and then set eyes upon Christina's limp form.

"We have to get her to the hospital, and quickly," he said gravely. I nodded, praying that Christina would be okay. The stranger must have sensed my concern, for he said reassuringly, "She should be alright, as long as she gets medical attention at once." Feeling a tiny bit relieved, I tried to lift Christina by myself, but my mysterious strength had vanished as quickly as it had appeared. "Let me help," the stranger said, and together we lifted her up.

"How far away is the hospital?" I asked anxiously.

"A couple blocks. My name's Austin, by the way." "Leigh."

"Nice to meet you, Leigh," said Austin with a

dazzling smile. "I'd shake your hand but I'd prefer not to drop Christina here."

I gasped. "You know her?"

He nodded in a serious sort of way. "We went to school together for years. How do you know her?"

I glanced around nervously, trying to think of a way to explain. "Um...she..she called me, like, I was just sitting in my bedroom looking at my mirror..and I heard her voice.."

Austin's green eyes grew large, and he nearly dropped Christina. "You're a mortal??"

"I suppose that's the term for earthly beings around here..." I responded slowly.

"Why were you glowing like that, then? Only Vitreusians have that glow about them!"

I stole a glance at my hands, and realized they no longer glowed! I looked back at Austin, whose face was rapidly becoming pale. "Tell me more, please," he said, a faint look about him that made me worry he'd let go of Christina.

So I did, about coming to Vitreusia with Christina, how she'd entered the building and I'd gone after her, my strange five-minute superhuman strength, the burning feeling and the yellowish glow.

He listened without a word, his features drawn and nervous. We were at the doors of the hospital by the time my story had come to a close. Before we entered the brick building, he looked me in my blue eyes and said in a voice that shook, "I must speak with you later."

For a while after Austin and I saw Christina

safely into one of the hospital rooms, we were kept busy helping the doctors and nurses out, as there was an overload of patients. We washed instruments, ran around and grabbed bandages and ice water for what seemed like an eternity.

When the influx of injured Vitreusians had come to a halt, Austin and I made our way to where Christina lay in a very clean hospital bed, breathing without any difficulty, but still unconscious. I glanced at the clock, one of the only furnishings in the austere hospital room. It had been three hours since we'd carried Christina through those double doors.

My thoughts were interrupted by Austin's voice. "Leigh..I must tell you something."

"I'm listening," I replied, my blue eyes shifting to Christina, then to Austin and back again.

"Vitreusia..is a very old world, with lots of history," began Austin. "It has had times of peace and turmoil, security and uncertainty, beauty and horror. However, the historians have noticed a..pattern, if you will.

Throughout its history, whenever Vitreusia was in very deep trouble, a hero arose to rescue it from complete and utter destruction. Sometimes the heroes were Vitreusians. Other times a mortal rose to the challenge. but they all had one thing in common:that, even when faced with certain death, they said to themselves, 'there has to be some other way'."

My eyes widened. I had thought that very thought today, trapped in the burning building with Christina! "Then," Austin continued, "the hero would

13

experience a burning feeling, and become unusually strong. If they were mortal, they would glow just like a Vitreusian.

The episodes would be brief at first, but gradually get longer and longer, until the very makeup of the hero had changed. The historians say that even after Vitreusia had been saved, the hero's powers would never leave him or her...they'd become a permanent part of them."

I swallowed nervously, and Austin took a deep breath. "Obviously, Vitreusia is in a lot of trouble...but less obviously, Leigh, you are the one who is meant to save it." and everything faded to black.

III.

I awoke to Christina's voice. "Leigh...Leigh..wake up, Leigh." I tossed, turned, and tried to open my eyes. They seemed to be clamped shut. "Oh, Leigh.." Christina pleaded, anxiety creeping into her voice. "Please wake up." Slowly, very slowly, I opened my eyes.

"Christina...I had a terrible dream. I dreamed you were stuck in a burning building and...and.." I then noticed a small bump on Christina's head. "Oh..it wasn't a dream, was it?" I asked foggily.

"Nope! It was all real!" cut in a cool, clear voice. "Austin?!"

"Yep," he answered, coming into view. "You fainted as soon as I told you about your destiny, Leigh." "You've been unconscious for three days," added Christina. "We were beginning to think you wouldn't wake up."

I sighed. "Sorry. I'm not cut out for this hero stuff, I guess."

Austin smiled. "Nah, it's fine. This is totally normal. All of the heroes who knew their destiny beforehand either lost consciousness or went into shock after someone told them what they were meant to do and who they would become. You've just become one of that number."

I conjured up a grin, despite my inner turmoil. I had thought that there would be no problems here. Hadn't Christina said something to that effect? As if she'd read my mind, Christina spoke up. "Once you have done your job, Leigh, everything will go back to normal, and Vitreusia will be untroubled and peaceful once more."

Austin scowled. "Hey, I was going to tell her that."

Christina shrugged. "Sorry, history buff." I giggled softly, and Austin pretended to look hurt - but I could tell he wasn't at all. "Austin probably told you we went to school together," said Christina, "he was at the top of our history class from beginning to end."

I raised my eyebrows. "Whoa."

Christina nodded. "It's lucky you two met. Nobody could have explained your fate like he."

Austin smiled modestly. "There's no such thing as luck, Christina."

Christina groaned. "Ah, yes. That phrase was pounded into our heads from day one. 'There's no such thing as luck'."

Austin arose. "Listen, I hate to break this up and all, but our world is being destroyed right now, and Leigh needs to save it as soon as possible."

I gulped. *What? We were going out?* Out into the chaos, destruction, horror? Christina and I had just made it out by the skin of our teeth, and we were just going to walk out into that mess like there was no danger whatsoever? I started to panic. *There has to be some other way.* And I started to feel strong again, to glow again. Oh, darn. I really was Vitreusia's next savior.

Christina smiled at Austin, who looked to be numb with a mixture of shock and awe. "Snap out of it," she told him. "We need to take her to Zach." I was perplexed. Zach? Zach who? I thought I was going out to do my destined job!?

Austin acknowledged my confusion by saying, "Zach is the keeper of the necklace and dagger." Christina nodded to back him up. I was still puzzled.

"What necklace? What dagger?" I inquired.

Austin beckoned to me. "Come, I'll tell you on the way," he said. "So," Austin started as the three of us walked through the chaos of Vitreusia that I was (so they said) meant to save, "Ever since Vitreusia's first great tribulations, there has been a special dagger and necklace, meant for the hero who will arise." I glanced over at Christina, who bobbed her head, silently telling me that Austin was correct. "The necklace will glow when you are in your stronger form, which, as I said before, will ultimately replace who you were previously." I swallowed nervously, and Austin went on, "The dagger is to be used only in your greatest time of need. Until then, you must always have it with you."

I took a deep breath. So much to remember! Who would have thought that being a champion would be so complicated? Then Christina knocked at the door of a small (yet tidy) hut. The door was opened by a young man, who looked to be about seventeen or eighteen, just a year or so my senior. "Yes?" he inquired cautiously, his hazel eyes darting around with extreme vigilance.

I noticed in that moment that my transformation had ceased already. Then recognition took over his facial features. "Christina! Austin!" he exclaimed, hugging them both. "It's so good to see you!" Then he saw me. "Who is this?"

"This is Leigh," Christina spoke up. "Leigh, this is Zach, privileged bearer of the necklace and dagger." Austin breathed in heavily, and then spoke, "Zach, this is Leigh, Vitreusia's next liberator."

Zach's eyes widened and he ran his fingers through his golden brown hair. "Oh! Ever since I was appointed keeper of the necklace and dagger I hoped that Vitreusia's next savior would be a mortal, and it is so!" It was then that I noticed Zach did not glow like Austin and Christina, meaning he must be human as well. "Come in, please come in!" said Zach, his face glowing with admiration.

And we did. I followed Zach to a secret chamber, where the necklace and dagger were displayed in a heavily secured glass case. It took about five minutes for him to unlock the case, and then he hung the dagger at my side, and with trembling hands clasped the necklace around my neck. A feeling of warmth and strength rushed over me, and I fell to my knees (I do not know why). The next thing I knew Zach said, "Rise, Leigh Kaitlyn Kline, twenty-third in the line of Vitreusia's heroes!"

I got to my feet and gave the necklace and dagger a quick once-over. On the necklace was a golden shield, which hung from a golden chain, and on top of the shield two bejeweled swords were crisscrossed. The dagger had a golden hilt, which was also adorned with gems of all colors. The hilt, in addition, had intricate swirls and curls that were raised, giving it extra texture. Slowly, I pulled the dagger out of its sheath, and its silver blade glinted in the dim lighting of the secret chamber.

Zach watched in wonder, his hazel eyes glittering with complete and utter bliss. As I put the dagger back in the scabbard, I noticed my clothes had changed. My designer jeans and pink polo had been replaced with a yellowish orange robe, unlike any I'd ever seen. The material was light and flowing but somehow sturdy, and I felt that I could run in it quite easily.

Zach motioned to me, saying, "Let's go. Christina and Austin are waiting." I nodded and followed him out of the chamber. When they saw me, Austin nearly fell over, but Christina steadied him (although she did not look as if she was feeling very strong herself). "Shall we go?" inquired Austin, slicking back his azure hair in a quick motion.
My palms began to grow sweaty. "Now?" I asked.
"Yes, now," replied Austin. "I...I'm not sure I'm

ready." I said, my voice trembling nervously. "I think I need to know a little more." Austin's green eyes shifted to Christina, giving her one, quick, questioning glance.

"What are your questions?" he asked with a significant amount of hesitation. "How did Zach come to be the keeper of the necklace and dagger? He's mortal like I am, right?"

Zach nodded. "Yes, Leigh, I certainly am."

I looked at Austin, pleading silently for him to explain. "I'll try to make this quick," he said. "When Vitreusia's first hero died, they had no further need of the necklace and dagger. Not knowing if these cherished items would be desirable in the future, the people of Vitreusia sought someone to keep them hidden away in a safe, secret place until, and if, they were needed. They realized quite quickly, though, that no one could touch these honored assets. It was as if an invisible force field had been placed around them, and nobody could penetrate it. Then, as the townspeople discussed what to do, a young girl crept up and picked up the dagger and necklace. Taking this as a sign, the people of Vitreusia appointed the girl the first keeper of the dagger and necklace. She died after many years, and was succeeded by two other bearers before Vitreusia's next crisis.

So whenever a hero of Vitreusia or a bearer dies, the townspeople gather together to assign a new keeper. Zach came to Vitreusia when he was little more than fourteen. He'd resided here for a year when he became the seventy-ninth guardian of the necklace and dagger. Is this what you needed to know?"

"Yes, thank you Austin," I replied, my curiosity satisfied for the moment. Zach sprung towards the door with an amount of energy that rivaled a caffeinated three-year-old. "Let us go!"

IV.

Together we darted out of the hut, and I felt the burning feeling again. "What's happening?" I inquired of Austin, who was running at my side. "I didn't think that special thought but my powers are returning!!"

"After the first few times, you don't have to think of that particular phrase—the alteration can occur at any instance." "Good to know," I replied sarcastically, panting. "Where exactly are we going??"

"The enemy was last seen by Glass Mountain," said Zach. "We must confront him!"

"I don't know if I'm ready!" I exclaimed.

"You must be!" cried Christina. "You're our only hope, Leigh! If anyone can save Vitreusia, it's you—only you are capable!"

I sighed. "No pressure."

We continued towards the iridescent peak of Glass Mountain. As we approached the foundation of it, our foursome slowed down. "You should stay here," I said to my friends. "I can't let any of you get wounded. I would never forgive myself."

"No!" contradicted Zach, putting his foot down. "I have waited for this for years - if I get wounded or if I die, so be it! I have seen a mortal arise to save Vitreusia, the moment for which I have lived and breathed, and the one I have for so long hoped to see. I will be delighted to die defending the champion I have longed to see for years—overjoyed!" he took my hand and kissed it with the utmost respect and reverence. "I will defend you to the end, Leigh." My hand flew up to my hair in a tense gesture. I did not know how to respond to this incredible valor.

Christina spoke up. "So will I."

"I will too," said Austin solemnly, and in one swift motion they were all on one knee before me. I took a step back, not knowing what to think of their eccentric behavior. It was as if I was their queen! Well, in a sense, I was, I suppose. Still, it made me uncomfortable, them kneeling like that.

"Please rise, Zach, Christina, Austin." Zach made his hands into fists and crossed them over his chest, then arose, and Austin and Christina did the same. I stood there for a short moment, bewildered.

Austin whispered in my ear as he stepped forward to lead, "It's an ancient Vitreusian salute, reserved for heroes alone."

Then together we made our silent ascent of the mountain, each of us on guard and ready to fight for our lives (or, in Zach's case, my life—he did not seem to care much about his). As I climbed the mountain, I kept a sharp lookout, making sure I could see Zach, Christina and Austin at all times. I knew that they were both ready and willing to defend me, but that wouldn't stop me from feeling responsible.

All of the sudden I heard a whistling noise. I turned to my right (where the sound was coming from), and perceived an arrow hurtling towards me! I ducked, yelling, "Austin, Christina, Zach! Look out!" They all ducked, and the arrow flew into the ground and stayed there.

Christina reached over her shoulder and grabbed a wooden bow, made with extraordinary craftsmanship. She fitted an arrow to it and then continued walking. "I didn't know you were an archer," I said to Christina.

Zach laughed. "*Archer* would be too diminutive a term. She is the most accurate archer in all of Vitreusia."

"Wow," I mused. "That's amazing."

"What's even more amazing," cut in Austin, "is that she may be the greatest archer in the history of Vitreusia." Christina shook her head in humble disagreement.

"Either way, you are very well protected, Leigh," stated Zach, his left hand on the hilt of his sword (which I hadn't known he carried until now). Then the arrows began to fall thick and fast.

"Quick, behind this tree!" cried Austin, rushing over to it and whipping out his sword.

"What's going on?" I asked, almost out of

breath, between the running and my fear.

"The enemy," said Zach seriously. "We have reached—or are getting close to—his hideout."

"I must go alone," I said firmly. "This is too dangerous for you. Please, stay here and be safe. I will do this unaided."

Zach put a strong hand on my shoulder. "*No, Leigh!*"

I stepped back, stunned by his outburst. "You may have powers, but you are not invincible. If you fall all is lost! We must protect you as long as we are able and at all costs!"

"I can't let you do this," I said, my voice falling to little above a whisper.

"You *must*," disagreed Zach, his voice growing quiet but still unyielding.

I turned to Austin and Christina for help, but Austin said softly, "Zach is right, Leigh." Christina gave a brief nod, fitting another arrow into her bow.

Zach slowly drew out his sword. "Lead the charge, Austin," he said.

We all rushed up the mountain, dodging arrows (and, in Christina's case, letting some loose).

Our charge led us into a cave, which was dark and damp. Just as I was on the verge of suggesting that we should turn around, as this was not the enemy's lair, my necklace began to glow once more. "Look!" cried Christina. "A passage!"

We approached it, Zach and Austin clinging tightly to their swords, and Christina with her bow stretched taut. While we walked down it, we neither saw nor heard anything strange. There were only the stone walls, which seemed to stretch on forever in the yawning darkness of the cave. After a minute or so, we came upon a fire pit, with ashes piled up about six inches thick. "Someone has been in here recently," uttered Austin, his voice bouncing off the stone walls and creating an eerie echo.

"Yes," agreed Zach. "but who—and why?"

"We must find out," I said, cringing at the reverberation of my voice. On we strode, seeing almost nothing but each other, hearing almost nothing but our comrades.

Then Zach held up his hand. "Wait..listen." we all stopped and strained our ears.

"I don't hear anything," said Christina.

"Me neither," Austin cut in.

"It's...a really weird sound," said Zach. "Listen some more...we might hear it again." And we did, the four of us hardly daring to breathe. I surveyed the walls, still listening for the 'weird sound'. Then a different sound ripped through the cold, moist air of the cave. It was not a strange noise at all. In fact, I recognized it at once. **Christina's scream**.

V.

Zach blanched and held his sword at the ready. My hand flew to the hilt of my dagger involuntarily. "Austin!" yelled Zach. "Christina!" Neither of them responded. "Stay close to me," instructed Zach as he looked for our companions.

"Austin! Christina!" I hollered at the top of my lungs. The only response I got was my own echo. "What has happened to them?" I whispered, my heart pounding violently.

"I…I don't know," Zach responded. "They may have fallen into the hands of the enemy."

The thought was too much to bear. *"No!"* I shouted, making Zach jump. He put a hand on my shoulder.

"We'll find them, Leigh," he said, doing his best to sound hopeful. I could tell by the tremors when he spoke, though, that he was afraid we wouldn't be able

to find them…or worse, find them…*too late.*
Somehow, he knew that I knew this—I felt it. The
next thing he said was, "We need to get out of here.
I'm not sure how long your necklace will keep
glowing." I nodded in agreement. He was right.

We continued down the dark corridor vigilantly,
Zach clutching his sword so tightly that I was certain
that if I could see his knuckles they would be white.

We'd been walking for about five minutes when I
saw a sliver of daylight up ahead. Zach rushed
forward, brandishing his sword. I followed, my
orange-yellow robe flickering about like a flame that
was made of cloth.

Then Zach came to an abrupt stop, and put his
arm out, barring me from going any further. I ran into
him, and he held me back. "What are you doing?!" I
asked in confusion. He said nothing, but looked
downwards with his hazel eyes. I did the same, and
realized at once the reason for his actions. The edge
of the cave dropped off at a near 90-degree angle, and
sharp rocks covered the ground, which was a couple
thousand feet away. If Zach hadn't impeded me, I
would have plunged right off the cliff and fallen to
my death. "Thank you," I breathed, not knowing
what else to say.

"I'm doing the job I'm meant to do, and gladly at
that," he replied.

"What do we do now?" I inquired.

Zach took a deep breath. "We have to confront
the enemy, somehow, someway, and, most important
of all, quickly. Every second we wait increases the

chance of the two of us not being able to rescue Austin and Christina, or, perhaps, rescuing them too late."

"I know that, Zach," I answered. "You *know* I know that."

He sighed, nodded. "Listen, I may be one of the most skilled swordsmen in Vitreusia, but I'm not invincible-neither are you. However, you are the only one who can save this place."

"I know.." I moaned. This pressure was becoming impossible to stomach—even though my friends' intentions were good.

Zach continued, "so if I get trapped somewhere, or vanish like Austin and Christina, you mustn't try to rescue me. Save yourself. *Don't risk your life for me. It's not worth it.*"

I was near tears. "I couldn't *do* that to you, or Austin or Christina—I just couldn't! I can't just abandon you guys like that!"

Zach shook his head, his expression suggesting slight exasperation. I was flat out crying by now, the tears streaming down my face. "Leigh…don't get like this. *Please.*" I tried to check the tears, but they kept on pouring down in a torrent of saltwater.

"Think of it this way," he said. "If something like..what I just mentioned were to happen, the only way you can rescue us, or them, or me is to *not* do so right away. Escape, regroup, and *then* face the enemy. Okay?"

"Okay..I guess." I sniffed.

Zach squeezed my arm, a kind light in his eyes.

"You can do this. Come on, let's find our way down."

As it was impossible to climb down a cliff, Zach and I ascended further up Glass Mountain first. It was a hard, grueling climb, and I let out a sigh of relief when we reached the top. Then I gasped. The view was incredible. I felt like I had suddenly sprouted wings and taken flight. My thoughts were interrupted by Zach's voice. "Splendid, isn't it?" he asked.

"Oh, yes."

"This was one of the first things I did when I came here years ago—scale this mountain. I've done it many times since…it never fails to take my breath away."

We both stood there in silence for a short time, taking in the outlook. Then I had one of the worst episodes of word-vomit in my entire life. "Zach?"

"Yes?"

Before I could stop myself, the words tumbled out of my mouth. "You're amazing." His eyebrows knit together for a moment, and I immediately felt regret for my random (and extremely awkward) comment.

Then he surprised me by laughing softly and saying, "Well, you'd be one of the first to make *that* observation—not that it's necessarily true." Naturally, I was puzzled by this remark.

"What do you mean by that?"

Zach sighed. "Back home on Rhode Island…I had a lot of trouble. Most kids I went to school with hated me, and I still don't know why. I was tripped in the hallways, alone at lunch. It was..pure torture, day in and day out. One day after school, I was looking in a mirror and thinking to myself, 'wouldn't it be great if I could just walk through this mirror and leave this mess behind?' Then a voice called me…and here I am."

"Wow…I'm…sorry about that, Zach," was all I could say. "Don't you feel better here, though?"

Zach sighed again, rubbing the hilt of his sword. "Yeah, it's much better. I have great friends like Christina and Austin…and now you, of course." I wanted to accept this answer of his, but the hollow sound in his voice troubled me.

"What's wrong?"

He ran his hand through his light brown hair. "Leigh…I've never told anyone this, but I don't really feel like I belong here. Everyone's really nice to me and all, but I still feel kind of empty. It's probably just me, but I've always had that feeling ever since I came here, like I'm ridiculously out of my league."

"I'm sorry," I said. "You didn't have to tell me."

"I wanted to, Leigh. I just felt somewhere deep inside that if there was one person I could tell about this, it was you."

Those words knocked me off my feet. I had no idea how I could respond. Zach saved me the worry. "We should go," he said, heading down the mountain. I trailed him, still reeling from his statement. When we were in town, Zach asked around to see where the foe had last been seen. Nobody could tell us. Finally a girl with wavy navy hair and pale pink eyes informed us that my opponent was spotted by the Cliffs of Fate. We thanked her, and I asked Zach, "Where are the Cliffs of Fate?"

Zach answered my question by pointing to a large, grey mass in the distance. "Those are the Cliffs of Fate," he said, and a shiver ran up my spine.

VI.

We journeyed towards the forbidding cliffs, stopping for a few minutes in an orchard to refresh ourselves. Zach seemed to be getting tired. "Do you need to rest?" I asked. The last thing I wanted or needed was the loss of my only remaining companion. "I'm good," he replied, shaking off his fatigue.

"Are you sure?" I persisted.

"Yes," was his firm answer. We continued on, the cliffs growing closer with every step, looking more threatening with every passing moment. Soon their dark form was about a ten minute walk away. Zach halted and pulled his sword out of its sheath. Before advancing, he turned to me. "Leigh, remember what I said."

A lump arose in my throat. "I'll try," I choked. Zach's features were grim. "You must do more than just try, Leigh. *Remember what I said.*" I gulped.

He was the only friend I had left in this strange land—I could never bring myself to desert him like he asked when the time came! "Promise me you won't forget what I told you, Leigh," he said steadfastly.

I took a deep breath, and a couple of tears rolled down my cheeks before I eked out, "I promise."

He wiped away my tears in a gesture that was brief but gentle. He grabbed my hand and gave it a quick squeeze. "Don't worry about me, Leigh," he said. "Please."

The only response I could muster was a slight nod of the head. Then we began to walk towards the cliffs.

We made our way through a gorge, surrounded by dark rock on our left and right. My breathing became shallow, and I started to sweat out of fear and nervousness. I looked up just in time to see a wicked fork of lightning flash across the sky. My necklace began to glow, and the familiar burning feeling returned. Zach made no mention of it and continued to walk beside me in the shadows.

Out of nowhere, I heard a laugh. It was nothing like the maniacal laughs of the villains in movies. No, it was more horrible and alarming than all that mirth put together. I compared it to a combination of the roar of a lion and a crack of thunder. Zach started and looked up, and I vigilantly followed his gaze. A tall, muscular figure stood above us. The ghastly sound cleaved through the air again.

Then my adversary spoke, with a voice that sounded like the grinding of a knife. "It has been nice to meet you, 'hero of Vitreusia'," He mocked. "Or rather, *see* you, as you will not get close enough for us to actually meet." Just as he had spoken the last word, a cloud of arrows came rushing towards Zach and I. Without thinking, I dodged them with the agility of an Olympic gymnast. Zach did the same.

I had evaded the last one and was breathing a sigh of relief when I perceived an arrow headed straight for my chest. I stood there, frozen into place. There was no way that I could dodge this one. It was only a few feet away and getting closer every second. This time, there was no way out. I made peace with my fate, a silent tear trickling down my face. I had failed. I'd failed Vitreusia. I'd failed Austin, Christina, and Zach. Their world would be torn apart now that I, the destined hero, tasted defeat. "I'm sorry," I whispered under my breath, the arrow seconds away from piercing me. "So sorry."

Out of the blue, Zach rushed over to me, his face marked with solemnity. "I made a promise, and I intend to keep it. **I will defend you to the end, Leigh,**" he said soberly. And then…he leapt in front of me, shielding me from the arrow that was to bring about my demise.

As he fell to the ground, a bolt of lightning seemed to rip through me, rooting me to the spot. I breathed a few short breaths before dashing over to Zach's side. "Zach!" I cried. "Are you alright?"

He winced. "No, not really."

"Here, let me help you up," I said, as my foe let loose another terrible laugh.

"Leigh, no!" Zach answered, his face contorted with pain. I didn't listen to his request. I *had* to save him.

The last thing I thought I would ever do was lift Zach's tall, lanky frame, but I resigned myself to the task, picking him up and trying not to make his wound worse. "Don't do this, Leigh," Zach said. "Don't."

But I held on to him, running through the gorge as fast as I could go. I kept running, running, running…away from the cliffs and towards the town. I had to get him to the hospital before it was too late!

On and on I sprinted, the dreadful mirth of my adversary following me. I hurried on, towards the brick building Austin and I had brought Christina to after I'd rescued her..that memory now seemed dull and far away. Dashing up to the doors, I shifted Zach into one arm and used the other to knock on the door, which was locked. "Please! Open this door! This is an emergency!" I yelled as loud as I could. A nurse peeked out of a doorway, but she made no move to let me in.

Then I had an idea. I made my necklace visible, the golden shield glowing vibrantly. When the nurse saw this, she quickly opened the door.

"What is wrong?" she asked me, her lilac eyebrows knitting together.

The words came out in choked sobs. "My friend…he's been shot…with an arrow…please, call the doctors!"

The nurse's golden eyes widened. "This way,

hurry."

She led me to a secret floor, which all the doctors, nurses and patients had retreated to for safety. She explained the situation to the doctors, and immediately they rushed forward. The nurse grabbed a gurney, upon which I laid Zach, who had passed out during my rush to the hospital. His hazel eyes blinked open and settled on me. I prepared myself for a lecture, but it never came. Instead, he reached out and grabbed my hand. "Leigh.." he said, flinching (it must have hurt him to speak) as he did so, "Be strong. Be strong for me."

He gave my hand a quick squeeze and let his arm fall limply at his side as the doctors rushed him away. I crumpled into a nearby chair, burying my face in my hands.

VII.

The next thing I knew, I was being tapped on the shoulder. "Miss?" inquired a doctor with yellow eyes, orange hair and a serious expression.

"My name is Leigh," I said, not bothering to look up.

"I…I wish I could say otherwise, but your friend is…he's dead."

"No!" I murmured, my head dropping onto my knees.

"I'm very sorry," he said, adding, "we did all we could."

It was then that the tears began to flow without restraint. "Oh, no…" I sobbed. "Zach…"

The doctor snapped to attention. "What did you say?" I lifted my tear-streaked face.
"Zach…that was his name." The doctor's yellow eyes grew wide with dismay. "That young man was Zach?

The bearer of the necklace and dagger?"

I nodded.

"Oh," said the doctor, his visage taking on a shocked expression. "Oh, my. This is very unfortunate, indeed." I did not respond, and he quietly left the room.

I began to cry again, tears flooding down my face in a salty waterfall. The thought that Zach would never again be there to wipe them away did not help the matter. I was engulfed in grief—grief and guilt. Grief for my loss of an unparalleled friend and companion—and guilt that I hadn't saved him. *"You should have run faster,"* a voice piped up from somewhere within. I recognized it as the same voice that had tried to dissuade me from touching the mirror. *"You didn't try hard enough—you could have rescued him! Now you must go on alone-and it's all your fault!"* The last few words sapped the little mental strength I had left.

I continued to weep. I felt as if I would never, ever stop crying. I tried to take deep breaths to calm myself down, but when I attempted that, all the sorrow and pain and remorse that I was feeling came up and choked me so that I could hardly breathe.

I was a rather sorry looking hero, my black hair all disheveled and mussed up, my robe torn in several places, my eyes emitting countless tears. Austin and Christina had disappeared. Zach was dead. I had to face my rival all alone now. I *knew* I had to—it was my destiny, my only hope of ever seeing Austin or Christina again. But I wasn't sure I could do it. The horrific laugh of my enemy rang in my ears, and I shuddered. *"I can't do this all by myself!!"* I thought with a sob.

◆ ◆ ◆

I stayed that way for awhile—alone, sorrowful. I began to contemplate all that Zach had done for me in the short time that I'd had the privilege of knowing him. First off, he'd saved my life—twice, the first time by stopping me from running off the edge of a cliff, and, of course, taking the arrow that was meant for me the second time.

I shook my head slowly, calling to mind how well we had gotten along together. I also remembered what he'd told me about his life back on Earth or whatever they call it here. A blaze of anger flared up within me at the thought of the cruelties he'd endured at his school. He was far away from all that now, at least. I brought to mind what he'd said, looking down upon Vitreusia. *I don't really feel like I belong here. Everyone's really nice to me and all, but I still feel kind of empty. It's probably just me, but I've always had that feeling, like I'm ridiculously out of my league.* A tear trickled down my cheek as I thought to myself that, wherever he was now, he probably felt like he belonged there. But then, we'd had some pretty good chemistry—at least I thought so…would he feel like he belonged with me? I surely would never know the answer to that question. I recollected his last words: *Leigh..be strong. Be strong for me.*

I took a deep, shuddering breath. I had to be strong, like he said. Not just for Zach, but Christina,

Austin and all of Vitreusia. Everyone was counting on me to be strong. Zach had solicited for me to be strong with the last sentence he would ever speak. I brushed back my hair and wiped away the tears that hung on my face. I adjusted my robe and replayed Zach's final appeal in my head. *"I'll be strong, Zach,"* I thought as I headed for the doors of the hospital. *"I'll be strong for you, just like you asked."*

I walked upon the path to the Cliffs of Fate for the second time in less than 3 hours, but the difference between this time and the last two times was that now, I journeyed alone. My resolve began to weaken as I approached the orchard where Zach and I had paused at earlier. A flashback assaulted me. *"Do you need to rest?" "I'm good." "Are you sure?" "Yes."* I leaned against a tree, discouraged by my recollection.

I looked over towards the cliffs, and realized the lightning storm had ceased. Somehow I found the nerve to stand up straight and continue on my travels.

When I approached the gorge, my breathing became quick and shallow. All efforts to calm myself down seemed to go to waste. I suddenly understood that I was experiencing a sensation I'd only heard about—a panic attack. Something within me, however, gave me just enough strength to keep moving on.

I soon drew near where Zach had taken the arrow for me. My head felt like it was spinning, and all I could see was the image of Zach leaping in front of me and falling to the ground…I could hear myself asking him frantically, *"Are you alright?"* I could see his face, the way he cringed in pain when he replied, *"No, not really."*

As I gradually came out of my trance, I noticed that my opponent was nowhere to be found. I began to climb up the cliffs where they weren't very steep, and I was scratched and bruised in many places by the time I reached the top. There were some caves that looked as if they had been mines at one point in time. On one stone wall next to the entrances of the caves, there was carved three words: **Darren Von Fare.** I wondered at what they might mean.

After pondering that for a moment, I moved on, into one of the caves. I became nervous again, as this cave was very similar to the one Austin and Christina had gone missing in. I wandered through the dark passages, with only my necklace giving me light to see by. Then I came upon a large door that was made of steel. It was locked. I banged on the door, hoping for a response. Through the secure door I heard faintly, "Leigh! Is that you?" *That was Christina's voice!* I tried to bust through the door, but it was much too sturdy. I began to panic. How could I get in there? I had to get in there! I couldn't bear to lose any more of my friends!! *"Think, Leigh, think,"* I told myself. *"There's got to be some way you can get in there."*

Then I remembered something—Austin saying to me when we were on the way to Zach's little hut, *The dagger is to be used only in your greatest time of need. Until then, you must always have it with you.* I went over the situation in my head. Zach was dead. Christina, at least was still alive—I had no clue whether or not

Austin was still breathing. The enemy was sure to return soon. This situation was desperate enough, I decided.

I pulled the dagger out of its sheath and beat the door with it—but the door did not even dent. *"Wait a minute.."* I thought to myself. I took the dagger and inserted it into the keyhole. I gave it a quick turn—and the heavy, steel door opened!

I rushed into the ominous room, and there were Austin and Christina! "Austin! Christina!" I cried, overjoyed to see them again. But neither of them smiled or said a word. Christina hung her head, shaking it slowly. "What's wrong?" I asked, puzzled by their behavior. Out of the blue, something hit me, *hard*, taking the very wind out of me, pinning me firmly against the wall.

VIII.

I tried to get free, but my struggles were in vain. The person who held me against the wall laughed that horrible laugh…*the enemy!* My heart pounded as I studied him. He was, as I'd noticed previously, tall, thin and muscular. His eyes were an icy blue, and his hair was a sleek, shiny black. He spoke, the unnerving sound of his voice echoing throughout the cave. "So, we meet again," he said in that grinding voice, staring at me through narrowed blue eyes. "And this time shall be the last!" He held me fast with one arm and turned to Austin and Christina. "I hope you don't mind me taking over Vitreusia—because I'm about to do it!"

"I mind!" spoke Austin resolutely.

My opponent laughed again. "That doesn't really matter, does it? I'm going to gain control anyway! And my name will be carved **everywhere,** just like on the entrance to this cave!" I now knew what those words had meant—not that it helped me in any way, shape or form. Darren continued, "Maybe I'll make a museum out of this place. Everyone will want to see where the last 'hero of Vitreusia' was overpowered by yours truly!"

Indignation rose up within me, and I found my voice. "You haven't defeated me yet!" I argued with all I had.

His strong hands wrapped around my throat in a flash. "Not yet, you say!" he mocked as I fought back, trying to pry his hands away. "Well, I'm just about to do it. You know, I thought this 'hero' would be stronger, but I guess I overestimated the lame defenses of this world!" He chuckled manically. When he said *stronger*, I felt a stab deep within. *"I'm sorry, Zach,"* I thought, sadness stabbing into my heart. *"I tried so hard to be strong for you like you asked."*

Darren was still on a monologue. I managed to ignore most of it (partly because I was going to pass out in less than a minute). But there came a sentence I could not tune out. "I hope that kid who took the arrow for you isn't disappointed. He saved your life for nothing." *He was talking about Zach!* That did it. How dare he mock Zach's heroic deed! Filled with anger now, I thought, *"I will be strong!! I will be strong, Zach! I won't let you down!"*

With a sudden burst of strength, I tore Darren's hands from my throat and pushed him with such force that it sent him flying across the room. As Austin and Christina looked on in confused amazement, I yelled at Darren with all my might, "You will **not** take over Vitreusia! You will **not** defeat me! My friend didn't save my life for nothing, he saved it for **everything!**" Darren picked himself up off the floor, a dazed look on his clear-cut features. "You want to fight me?" I asked, with a chill in my voice that rivaled his. "Excellent. I'm stronger than you imagine me to be—and I *will* ultimately be victorious, **Darren Von Fare.**"

Darren shook off his hazy expression, his blue eyes narrowing and giving him a very dangerous look. He rushed at me, his fists clenched. He got closer and swung one powerful fist towards my face..but my lightning-fast reflexes kicked in and I grabbed his wrist and held it in an iron grip. I dealt him several punishing blows before he freed himself from my grasp. Darren ran to the other side of the room, as if trying to escape from me. I'd won! He'd given up!

Then a sword came swinging through the air. I ducked, lost my balance, and found myself on the floor. I rolled back and forth, dodging the blade several times before I was able to get back on my feet. I then kicked the hand in which Darren held the sword, and it flew out of his grip and into one of the walls with a loud *crash*. I wasn't ready for what came next—a swift uppercut that sent me reeling. I was on the floor again, Darren standing over me. I kicked his legs out from under him, and he fell with a heavy *thud*. I grabbed his arms and pinned them behind his back. I tore two strips off my robe and tightly bound his wrists. I wondered why he hadn't struggled, and then realized that he was unconscious. He must have hit his head on the ground. That explained the thud I'd heard.

Darren being taken care of for the moment, I dashed over to where I'd seen Austin and Christina. Their countenances were full of relief. "What do I do now?" I asked them.

"We have to take Darren back to where he came from," replied Austin. Darren gave a low moan.

"Let's go, then, before he wakes up!" I implored them. Austin's face was grim. "These," he said, rattling chains that bound his wrists, "Might be a bit of a problem."

Christina sat up straight, jangling her bonds. "I'm stuck, too." "Where's the key for them?" I inquired, glancing anxiously over at Darren, who had begun to stir.

"I don't know," said Austin, and Christina shook her head.

"I bet Darren does," I replied, heading over to where he lay prostrate on the floor.

"He doesn't know either," declared Austin, his green eyes solemn.

"What!?" I asked, panic rising in my voice.

"He just snapped these on us, Leigh," Christina stated softly. "He was never going to let us go."

"There's got to be some way I can get you guys out of here!" I cried.

Then I remembered. *The dagger.* I sprinted to where I'd left it on the floor. Using it, I cut Christina and Austin loose. The iron shackles still remained on their wrists, along with a few chain links, but when I made a move to try and get them off, Austin shook his head. "There's no time for that," he said. The three of us took hold of Darren, who still seemed a little out of it. We helped him up and walked out of the cave.

When we were out in the sunlight and fresh air again, Austin and Christina both managed a small smile. I guessed they hadn't seen daylight since they had disappeared in that cave. I noticed that they both had wounds on their foreheads, long slashes of red. Before I could ask them about their gashes, Darren broke free. He shoved Austin and Christina away and knocked me over with one quick blow. He kicked me, and I nearly slid off the cliff and to my death. I was able to grab the edge of the precipice, and I held on for dear life. Darren laughed sardonically and knelt down, his sub-zero blue eyes level with mine. "Goodbye, Leigh," he said as he prepared to push me over the edge. "It's been nice beating you."

IX.

As he reached out to thrust me off the overhang, I grabbed both his wrists, yanked, and flipped over him and onto the rock, landing on my feet. A yell rang out behind me, and I whirled to see what the sound was about. There was Darren, plunging towards the ground. I gasped as I realized that when I had jerked his arms, he had been propelled off the crag. I could hear the ghastly thump as he hit the ground and remained motionless. Not too long after that, his body vanished into thin air and was gone.

I turned away from the precipice and looked at Austin and Christina. "Are you two alright?" I asked. "Did he shove you into the rock really hard or anything?"

"We're okay," said Christina. "He didn't have to push either of us really hard—we're not all that strong right now, you know."

"Let's just say he didn't bother to feed the bait," put in Austin, attempting to make light of the grim detail. I was horrified.

"What about the gashes on your foreheads?" I inquired, wondering what upsetting back story was behind those.

"Oh, *those*," Austin said, reaching up to run his hand across the long red cut. "I nearly forgot about these suckers."

"He did that in the cave," spoke up Christina.

"That's right," said Austin. "He gave us a nice little staggering blow across our foreheads with his sword to stun us. It sure worked, I can tell you that."

"That's why I screamed," explained Christina. "Austin was standing next to me, and then I heard a *whoosh!* The next thing I knew he fell to the ground."

"That's...awful," I said, shuddering.

Austin shrugged. "It hurt like heck for awhile, but it's all over now."

Christina let out a deep breath. "Yes, thank goodness! I'm so glad that I at least had Austin with me. That period in time was unpleasant enough *with* company."

"Speaking of company," began Austin, "where's Zach?"

"Oh..." I leaned against the rock, weakened by grief. "He's dead," I said, the words heavy on my tongue.

Austin and Christina were shocked. It was as if I had simultaneously slapped them in the face. A tear rolled down Christina's cheek and splashed down onto the rock. Austin's eyes started to water, and he asked, "What happened?"

I inhaled heavily. "We were here—at the Cliffs of Fate, when Darren appeared above us and fired a multitude of arrows at us. We dodged all of them—at least I thought we had. Then I saw an arrow heading straight for my chest. It was too close for me to evade. I thought I was done for. Then Zach…leapt in front of me. He took the arrow…for me." I hadn't looked at Austin or Christina during the account, and I lifted my eyes to meet theirs.

Christina looked a bit dazed. Austin's head was slightly bowed, and the trail of a tear shone out on his face. "Did he…was he killed on the spot?" asked Christina tearfully.

I shook my head. "No. I picked him up and ran for the hospital, and the doctors tried to save him…but their efforts were fruitless."

"This saddens me greatly," said Austin, slowly lifting his head up. "However…I hate to say this, but…there's few better ways that he could've gone out." I gave him my best quizzical look. "For him, I mean," he said quickly. "You know what I'm getting at. He often told you he was willing to risk his life and even die for your sake."

"I see," I whispered.

"His name will be remembered forever," Austin remarked to himself. "His heroic deed will live on for millennia."

"He deserves it," I observed.

"Indeed he does," said Christina softly.

It was on this serious note that we began to make our way back to the village. We approached the village, which reminded me of a ghost town. There were no people in sight. "They must all still be in hiding," said Austin.

Christina smiled weakly. "We know how to take care of that," she said, and together they chanted at the top of their lungs, **"Exi, exi, lux est victor!"** I watched the village come to life, as if by magic. Everyone gathered around the three of us, and they seemed to be waiting for something. Austin climbed upon a nearby boulder and beckoned for me to join him. Still confused, I clambered to the top.

Then Austin said, "Ego tibi heros vicesimo tertio esti heroum de Vitreusia, Leigh Kaitlyn Kline!" The villagers immediately did the same salute that Austin, Christina and Zach had before we had gone up Glass Mountain, and they shouted as one, "Historia fit!" Austin then got down from the boulder, and I did the same.

"What was that all about?" I asked.

"I just announced you as the twenty-third hero of Vitreusia. That's all," replied Austin.

"Oh," I said, still not understanding very much.

"The festivities will begin almost immediately," declared Austin. "To be honest, I don't feel quite up to it."

"Me neither," agreed Christina. "Not with what's happened to us and…and Zach over the past few days."

"I think the three of us should talk it all out

before the feast tonight," Austin said.

"What do you think, Leigh?" inquired Christina.

I spoke, nearly choking on the lump in my throat. "I agree with both of you."
So we went to Christina's residence, a good sized, perfectly kept little house. We sat down in the cozy living room, and almost immediately Austin and Christina's poker faces evaporated, the expressions on their visages now suggesting grief and distress. "Are you two..okay?" I asked, concerned for my friends.

Christina ran her hand over the wound on her forehead. "Physically, yes, we'll be alright. Mentally.." she sighed. "Not so much."

"Please explain," I pleaded.

Austin and Christina exchanged a quick but meaningful glance. "Leigh," began Christina, "You probably figured out why Darren captured us—to lure you into his lair."

"Yes, I realized that," I answered, wondering what she was leading up to.

"Like I told you before, he never intended to let us go," she said.

Austin spoke up now. "He was an arrogant, cruel, nasty fellow, that Darren. He often went into monologues about how you would fall right into his trap and then he'd take over Vitreusia…and of course Christina and I didn't think that would happen, and we told him that." He began to roll up his sleeve. "Well, good effort—bad idea."

"What do you m—" I started to ask, and then I saw the gashes on his forearm.

I clapped my hand over my mouth to keep myself from screaming. "Oh, Austin, how *horrible!*" I exclaimed. "Christina, did he do that to you, too?" I asked, not really wanting to know (but I *had* to know).

"No," Christina replied. "He would have, but..but Austin took mine for me."

For the first time since we'd been reunited, Austin laughed. "You should've seen his face, Leigh. He was absolutely shocked. Apparently chivalry wasn't an ideal quality in that twisted mind of his."

"That doesn't surprise me," I scoffed. "He thought Zach was an idiot." Then an unpleasant thought occurred to me. "Do you have those on the other arm, too?"

Austin gave a feeble laugh. "Ha! Of course. He's a thorough chap, that Darren."

I buried my head in my hands. "I'm *so* sorry. I should have come sooner."

"Don't blame yourself, Leigh," said Christina. "You had your troubles too."

"Poor Zach," remarked Austin sadly. "He was such a nice guy."

"That's the truth," I whispered.

"Leigh," Christina started, "When Austin and I were all locked up in that old mine, he remarked to me that you arguably had the most hardship out of all the heroes of Vitreusia-and that...that you might not be able to overcome it. That was a terrifying thought—because if you didn't defeat Darren, we were done for. Obviously Austin didn't know about Zach. So you, Leigh, are probably the most remarkable rescuer Vitreusia has ever had."

"Thank you," I said, "but Zach deserves a lot of credit. If it weren't for him, Vitreusia would have been torn apart."

We all were silent for a moment, calling our fallen friend to mind. "Just to conclude, Leigh," said Austin after we'd been still for a minute or so, "Christina and I will be okay—we just have to heal, I guess. We'll probably pay a visit to the locksmith tomorrow to get these chains off. It'll take a little while for us to recover from this..ordeal. Don't worry about us too much, though. Just give us some time." He reached over and squeezed Christina's hand, and Christina gave him a grateful smile. Then a bell began to ring. It had a strong, deep, powerful sound. Austin and Christina stood up. "Let's go," said Austin. "We shouldn't miss the main festivities."

X.

The three of us approached a large house, from which came the sounds of merriment. Austin took a deep breath and knocked on the door. It was opened almost immediately, by the same girl who had told Zach and I where Darren could be found. She smiled a dazzling smile, her pink eyes glittering joyfully. "Austin! Christina! I'm so glad to see you!" Then she looked at me, and her eyes widened with recognition. "Leigh! It is an honor to see you again!"

"Thank you," I replied. "I don't believe I know your name...?"

"Oh! Yes!" she said. "That would be helpful, wouldn't it? I'm Sabrina."

"Well, Sabrina, I'm glad that I'm able to meet you in a less serious circumstance."

"The feeling is mutual," she replied in a friendly way. Then concern flashed across her face. "Where is

Zach? Wasn't he with you?" I turned my sob into a cough and looked to Austin and Christina for help.

"Zach has, unfortunately, passed away," Austin said soberly.

Horror took over Sabrina's pretty face. "How awful! He will be sorely missed."

"Indeed he will be," murmured Christina.

"Well!" said Sabrina, smiling again (although less genuinely this time). "Won't you come in?"

So we did. The place was a little overwhelming at first. It looked to me that there were a good three hundred people in the building, most of them Vitreusians. A large table filled most of the room. As I made my way to the head of the table (that's where Austin said I was supposed to sit), a hush gradually fell over the room. Excited whispers could be heard as I sat down in the intricately carved chair at the head of the table. Then glasses of an orange liquid were brought out.

Austin got up from his chair (he and Christina were the two people who sat closest to me), raised his glass, and said, "To the twenty-third hero of Vitreusia!" A cheer swept through the room, a cheer so loud I could've sworn it shook the mansion's ancient walls. Austin motioned for me to get up. "Just make some sort of speech," he whispered to me. "It doesn't have to be long or fancy."

I arose. "Thank you. I am just as pleased to be celebrating this victory as you are." Austin gave me an approving nod, and I went on: "Although I am the one who wears the glowing necklace and has the dagger hanging at my side, I am not the one who *truly* saved Vitreusia." A confused hum spread through the crowd, and both Austin and Christina gave me inquiring looks.

I started to choke up as I said, "I'm sure that all of you know who Zach—the necklace and dagger's seventy-ninth keeper—is. He saved my life—by sacrificing his own. If it weren't for him, Vitreusia would have been doomed. I may have defeated Darren Von Fare, but Zach deserves some credit, too." Tears now flowed freely down my face. I regained control of my voice, raised my glass, and cried, "To Zach!"

Austin and Christina's eyes gleamed with looming tears as they repeated with the assembly, "To Zach!"

Now Christina got up from her seat. "I would like to acknowledge a loyal friend and companion, who stuck by me through the most difficult time in both of our lives. Austin, here's to you." I gave Austin a half hug, and Christina beamed at him as the mass repeated, "To Austin!" Austin arose again and said with a grin, "To a Vitreusian with a lot of courage and a very pretty face. I love you, Christina." The room fell silent as Christina blushed and went over to embrace Austin. Then everyone raised their glasses and gently knocked the glass of the person to their left. A feast followed, a lengthy celebration of my success in defeating one of Vitreusia's most formidable foes.

Afterwards, most of the people stayed to mingle,

including Christina, Austin and me. I had my hand
shaken by grateful Vitreusians countless times, and
Austin and Christina introduced me to many of their
friends. It made me both happy and sad to see Austin
and Christina holding hands, leaning on each other,
teasing back and forth. I was happy that they 'clicked'
the way they did. But I was saddened as well, because
I knew that Zach and I could have been doing
something similar tonight—had he been alive.

This thought was pushed from my mind when I
heard Christina say, "Leigh, we'd like you to meet our
good friend Lillian." I looked up. The woman they'd
just introduced me to was about five foot eight and
somewhat heavy-set. I knew I'd seen her before, and
when her golden eyes sparkled as I shook her hand I
remembered. "Lillian works at the hospital," said
Christina. "She's a wonderful nurse."

"I know she is," I said, and the three of them
looked a little confused. Tears came up in my throat
as I said, "We've met before, Lillian and I have. She
opened the door for—for Zach and me."

Lillian drew in a sharp breath. "I knew I'd seen
you before! I'm so sorry about your friend."

"So am I," said a vaguely familiar voice. I looked
to see who had spoken, and recognized the same
doctor who'd broken the news of Zach's death to me.
He shook my hand firmly, saying, "I wish I could
have done more."

"You both did everything you could," I said,
looking them both in the eye. "and I thank you
sincerely for that." They both nodded gravely and bid

us farewell, congratulating me on my triumph.

Not long after that, Austin, Christina and I left the house. The three of us walked together for awhile, and then Austin had to go a different way to get to his house. He gave me a quick hug. "See you tomorrow, Leigh."

Then he turned to Christina, and kissed her on the top of her head. "I'll see you in the morning."

"Okay," replied Christina in her soft, silky voice, and we continued on to her dwelling. Before I fell asleep that night, a good many silent tears slipped down my face. I'd won the battle I was meant to win...but I'd lost an irreplaceable friend in the process.

XI.

I awoke to Christina gently shaking me. The chains had (thank goodness) disappeared from her wrists. Her pretty face looked much less drawn and worried than it had yesterday. She gave me a clean robe that (unlike the one I had on) was not torn. "Just come to the kitchen when you're ready," she said as she exited the room. I changed quickly and headed for the kitchen, where Austin sat at the table. His chains had vanished also. I presumed that the two of them had gone to the locksmith's together, letting me rest.

Austin got to his feet to greet me. "Bonum mane, Leigh," he said. I was confused.

Christina translated swiftly, "Good morning."

"Oh!" I said, feeling rather stupid. "Bonum mane to you, too, then." Christina got me a hot drink. It had a warm, spicy aroma, and when I took a sip I could feel the warmth slipping down my throat.

"Leigh," said Christina, "We have to show you something—Austin and I do—and then...well, you have a decision to make."

I swallowed uneasily, and Austin smiled, setting my mind partly at ease.

"Don't worry, Leigh," he assured me.

They waited until I finished my drink, and then we left Christina's house. Austin and Christina led me to a part of town I'd never seen before. Suddenly Christina whispered something to Austin, and he covered my eyes with his hands.

"We're getting close," he explained. We walked for about ten more minutes, and then stopped short. Austin removed his hands from my eyes. I gasped as I took in what was in front of me. It was a statue, which looked to be carved of marble. It was on a large, square, deftly embellished platform, also made of marble. The figures were life-size and carved with the utmost detail. The reason why I gasped, though, was because of *who* the statue was of.

It portrayed Zach and I, back to back, looking over our shoulders at each other. Zach's sword was drawn, as was my dagger. I studied the memorial more closely. Not a single characteristic had been overlooked, from the part in Zach's hair to the glow of light around my necklace. "It's beautiful," I said, tears coming to my eyes. "Thank you. How did you manage to do something like that in just one night?"

Austin grinned. "Anything's possible when you have the help of all of Vitreusia—not to mention talented carvers who can carve through marble as if it's mere ice."

I shook my head in amazement. "How can I thank you enough?"

"No, Leigh," Austin corrected me, "The real question is, how can *we* thank you enough. You saved our world—maybe not singlehandedly, but you still saved it."

"I guess so," I agreed.

"Before we go," began Austin, "There's one more thing. This inscription," and here he pointed to some letters carved in the side of the statue's platform, which were written in a different language, "Says, 'Leigh Kaitlyn Kline, the twenty-third hero of Vitreusia, and Zach Dean Johnston, the necklace and dagger's seventy-ninth keeper. Friends to the end, together they liberated Vitreusia from Darren Von Fare. Their valor will be revered evermore.'"

I gave them both tight hugs. "Zach would say this is too much," I said, "but I say he completely deserves it."

We gazed upon the monument in silence for a few short moments, and then Austin said, "Leigh, the time has come…for you to make a difficult choice."

My heart jumped into my throat. "And what is that?"

Austin took a deep breath. "Leigh, you must decide—will you stay here, in Vitreusia? Or will you return to Terra?"

"Terra?" I repeated, confused.

"Oops. I meant Earth," said Austin apologetically.

"What would happen if I did?" I asked.

"You would retain your special powers, and your—er, Vitreusian glow will be sporadically visible. You will take both the necklace and dagger with you. They will be invisible to all but you."

"Hmm," I said, thinking this over.

"Also," spoke up Christina, "You have been here for the equivalent of eighteen days on Earth. If you return, you will have not experienced those eighteen days directly. You will have memories of those eighteen days that will appear suddenly in your mind upon your return."

"And what if I stay here?"
"You'll live in the manor built specifically for Vitreusia's saviors, and essentially be one of us."

I thought over my choices, and as I did so, Austin added, "and two more things. If you stay here, you may only travel back to Earth once, and for only a day or less, no more. If you try to go to Earth again, you will die." I was shocked.

"All Vitreusians are like that, Leigh," said Christina. "If you choose to stay, you will be considered a Vitreusian."

Austin nodded. "Christina is right. The second thing I must tell you is that if you return to Ter—Earth, you will be able to come and go from Vitreusia as you like. This is because you are a hero of Vitreusia, and we cannot cut you off from our world."

"If you were not one of Vitreusia's liberators, you would only be able to return every two Earth weeks," explained Christina.

I thought everything over as thoroughly as possible, my eyes shut tight. I debated with myself whether I should stay—or leave. Finally I opened my eyes. I turned to Austin and Christina, my mind made up. "I will go back," I said.

◆ ◆ ◆

I stood in the void, the necklace hanging around my neck, the dagger at my side. This was the place where my adventures in Vitreusia had begun, and it was here that they would end—for now. Austin and Christina were next to me. I gave both of them one last hug. "Do you remember the chant I taught you to get back here?" asked Christina.

"I know it by heart," I assured her.

"Good."

"Goodbye, Leigh," said Austin. "I hope to see you soon. Good luck."

"Yes, good luck," concurred Christina. Then they began to chant, and the darkness started to swallow them up. It enveloped them completely, and the sound of their voices, joined in perfect harmony, began to fade slowly away. The thin, cold darkness surrounded me once more. I wondered how I would return to my life on Earth, because I was certain now that my visit to Vitreusia had reached

The End.

H. R. KASPER

Part II: Hunted

"Leigh, you are in great danger."

I.

My eyes blinked open, and I found myself in a
strange, light blue room. Then I realized that the
room wasn't strange at all—it was my new bedroom
in our house in Missouri. How could I have
forgotten? I lay in bed for a little while longer,
thinking over the strange dream I'd had..about a
mysterious world called Vitreusia..it had seemed so
genuine. I wished that those incredible adventures
had been reality. With a sigh, I got out of bed—*wait!*
Something was hanging heavily at my side. I looked
down, and *there was the dagger,* in all its bejeweled
finery. *It hadn't been a dream, after all!*

I reached up and felt around my neck for the
necklace, which was also there, glowing with a soft,
warm light. I began to experience a distinctive mix of
emotions—happiness that Vitreusia hadn't been a
dream, but then a pang of grief over Zach's death.
But I could not stand there in my pajamas forever. I
had to get ready for school—my third day of it, to be
exact. As Christina had said, I had memories of the

first and second days, and neither had gone badly.

A half-hour later, I got my hot pink backpack out of my room and walked into the kitchen. I experienced the odd feeling of seeing a sight you've never *really* seen before, but remember setting eyes upon. The kitchen was pleasant, painted a cheery green. The appliances were stainless steel, and spotlessly clean. I decided that it wasn't nearly as nice as the kitchen we had back in California. My dad had left for work, so only my mom saw me take in the kitchen. She watched me, one dark eyebrow raised in curiosity. "Leigh, are you alright?" she asked. "You're acting like you haven't seen the kitchen yet!" Well, I actually *hadn't*, but I wasn't about to tell her that.

I produced a fake laugh (something I'd become very good at in the past few months). "Oh, sorry. I was just zoning out a bit—thinking about that speaker who's coming to school today." Another weird feeling—hearing yourself say something that you didn't *really* know (all of the sudden my life had become one huge paradox).

As I prepared myself some scrambled eggs, mom asked, "And this speaker, what is his or her name?"

"Zach Johnston," I replied, shocking myself with my own words. *Zach Johnston!* A tear slid off my face and into the pan, sizzling into steam the moment it touched the hot surface.

"Leigh, are you *sure* everything's okay?" My mom asked, for she'd seen the solitary yet significant tear.

"Leigh, snap out of it!!" I scolded myself as I scooped the eggs onto a plate and said, "Yeah Mom,

I'm fine..just a little homesick I guess."

"Okay, dear," said my mom, putting on her reading glasses and opening up the paper.

When I sat down at the table, she said from behind the paper, "I hear this Zach Johnston is quite the speaker." At the sound of the name of the young man who saved my life, I nearly choked on my eggs. *"I've got to get this under control,"* I thought as I replied, "Oh, really?"

Mom took off her reading glasses and put down the paper. "Yes, I hear he's booked for Red Ribbon Week already—not surprisingly, because his talk on bullying is phenomenal." Again, I was shocked, but this time I kept my emotions on the inside. I remembered Zach telling me about the nasty way he was treated at school. *"Most kids I went to school with hated me, and I still don't know why. I was tripped in the hallways, alone at lunch."* It seemed impossible, but I couldn't quell the hope that was rising up inside of me-could it be that Zach had **come back from the dead?!**

II.

My heart beating rapidly in anticipation, I walked into school. Zach's speech would take place at a quarter to two, forty-five minutes before the end of the school day. My mind was ablaze with interest, so much so that I struggled to focus during classes. It was quite embarrassing to be caught 'sleeping', especially as the new girl at school.

At last, the principal came over the PA system. "All students please report to the school auditorium." I got up from my seat with a sigh of relief and quickly left the classroom. Taking short, swift strides, I was one of the first to enter the auditorium. I took a seat in one of the front rows and set my backpack down at my feet…and I waited. Slowly the room began to fill with high-schoolers, and after I'd been in my seat for nearly ten minutes, a young man came onto the stage and tapped the microphone a couple times to test it. I struggled for breath. Neatly styled light brown hair..a tall, lanky frame..and I could *just* make out the—**hazel eyes!** It was all I could do not to run onto stage and embrace my resurrected friend.

At the end of the speech (which was, as Mom had said, incredible), the students were invited to have a word with the young activist. Only a few of those in the auditorium took advantage of this opportunity, and I was one of them. I took deep breaths in a futile effort to calm myself down as I waited to speak to a person I'd thought I would never see again. The girl in front of me, a petite blonde, said to Zach, "that was amazing. Keep up the good work." She shook his hand firmly and left, her head held high.

I wiped away the tears that had come to my eyes and eked out, "Zach! How did this happen?? I..I thought I'd never see you again!!"

He looked at me inquiringly, his hazel eyes showing great bewilderment. "I'm sorry?" he said, the very picture of mystification.

"Zach," I said breathlessly, "It's me, Leigh. Don't you remember who I am??" He squinted for a moment, his eyes blank, eyebrows knit together.

"I don't believe we've met," he said, kindly but decisively. I swallowed the plea that was rapidly rising in my throat and said with all the dignity I could muster, "I—I'm sorry, I guess I mistook you for someone else." I picked up my backpack and slung it over my shoulder. "That was a wonderful speech," I said as I hurried away, my face hotter than Orlando in July.

"What a horrible day," I remarked silently to myself as I got into Mom's green Jeep. When we got home, I tore up the stairs and went straight to my room, where I closed and locked the door. I fingered the necklace, which shone as warmly as ever. My mind was a steel trap, in which questions of all sorts whirled violently around in one huge, overwhelming vortex. *Why didn't he recognize me? What's wrong with him? Why is he even alive in the first place? Or does he have an identical twin-?* The most disturbing query of all kept arising in the disarray that had overwhelmed my mind. ***Am I crazy?!?***

A knock at the door interrupted my thoughts.

"Leigh? Is everything all right?" I took a deep breath and replied,

"Yeah, I'm fine Mom."

"Okay.."

I had no desire to explain today's events. Besides, I wasn't even sure if I could do it without either mentioning Vitreusia or sounding like a lunatic.

I did some of my homework, but I did more thinking about the day's events than work, so I still had about ninety minutes' work left when it was time for dinner. I came into the kitchen and saw that we were having pizza—for the third night in a row. I ate two slices and put away my plate. Mom saw that I was finished and asked, "Leigh, would you help me move around the furniture in the family room? I thought of a better arrangement."

"Okay Mom." Furniture moving would be no big deal now that I possessed superhuman strength!

"Here, Leigh, take the other end." And I did.

I lifted up the sofa easily—almost too easily. It was so light that I nearly hit myself in the face when I hoisted it up! Mom was surprised and a little concerned. "Since when are you so strong, Leigh?" she asked, trying to hide her unease with a smile. I laughed and shrugged as we moved the sofa into its new spot. The room was rearranged in no time, and I headed back to my room, playing with my necklace.

I got out my vocabulary homework and sat down on my bed to give it a once-over. It was a piece of cake—I'd known all these words since seventh grade (drama club probably had something to do with my extensive vocabulary). I began writing definitions of words, and I came to 'sheath'. I looked down at my dagger, which was in its sheath, and I pulled it out to look at it.

I laid it across my lap, one hand on each end of it. I admired the bejeweled hilt, memories coming back to me by the minute. I recalled Zach, hanging the dagger at my side. I remembered unlocking the door to where Darren had kept Austin and Christina prisoner...cutting off the chains which held them fast. I was so absorbed in thought that I did not notice my mom had walked into the room. "Leigh?" she said, her voice startling me so that I jumped and the dagger fell to the floor with a *clang,* "What are you doing?"

"Just my homework, Mom," I answered, hoping she hadn't heard the dagger fall to the ground.

Her blue eyes glimmered with worry and doubt.

"It looked really odd…your hands just hovering in the air like that. It was like you were..I don't know, but it looked rather strange." I gave her my best I-don't-know-what-you're-talking-about look. She waved her hand. "Never mind..I'll leave you alone now." And she left the room, the troubled expression still on her face.

"I am in for it now," I told myself as I finished up my work. But Mom didn't mention it the rest of the night. I was still awake when she went to bed, and she came in my room and closed the blinds (something I always forget to do). She turned and looked at me, and her hand clapped over her mouth, as if to stifle a scream. "Leigh—you're *glowing!*"

"I am?" I asked, doing my best to act clueless. Mom was not convinced. **"Why are you glowing like that??"**

"Must…be…that new lotion," I muttered, wrapping the blankets around me tightly. She asked no further questions, but left the room quickly.

I woke up the next morning, got dressed, and ate a hasty breakfast.

As I headed for my homeroom, I resolved to be very careful of my superpowers—I had no idea what would happen if I took things too far.

But then in computer lab, Mr. Elwood needed boxes of printing paper and a couple new printers moved—and I couldn't resist. I lifted the boxes with ease while nearly everyone else (except for the super-muscular football players) struggled with their loads. As I sat down at my desk, I noticed that Mr. Elwood was looking at me in a confused, suspicious way. Then, in science, I caught a beaker in mid-air (thanks to my now superior reflexes). Miss Hogan looked surprised, but said nothing. The worst of all, however, was when Mr. Bonnell turned off the lights to show us a slideshow of pictures from his recent trip to Greece, and *I glowed*. "Hey, Leigh's glowing!" exclaimed John Rivers, and the whole class turned to look. Mr. Bonnell's face turned ashen and he stared in disbelief. For nearly a whole two minutes, nobody moved. Then the warm, yellowish glow that emitted from me faded away, and the class continued, although Mr. Bonnell's voice shook for the rest of class.

Thankfully, Mr. Bonnell was my ninth period class, so I walked out of the room, my strides long and almost hurried. I'd convinced Mom that I knew the way to school well enough now and could drive myself just yesterday, so I could make a quick getaway. As I pulled out of the school parking lot, I decided to stop by a café and have a latte while I did my homework (of which I only had about an hour's worth). I found a close parking spot, grabbed my backpack, and walked into the café—*Olive's Coffee Shop*. As I waited in line to place my order, I thought to myself that a person a little bit ahead of me in the line looked familiar. I suppressed a cry of astonishment when I realized that, standing in line, two people ahead of me, was *Zach Johnston!*

III.

My heart sped up as I gave my order and waited for it at the counter. By inexplicable coincidence, his order and mine were ready at the same time. Reaching out to grab our drinks, our hands bumped and our eyes met. For a moment, my blue eyes were locked with his hazel ones, and we gave each other an apologetic smile. I took my latte off the counter. "Leigh?" said Zach questioningly, making my heart give a leap of hope.

I squashed down the excitement that was rising up within me as I responded, "That's me."

A wave of satisfaction washed over Zach's face. "Good, I got it right. Weren't you the one who mistook me for someone else yesterday?"

A sharp pang of disappointment permeated my voice as I replied, "That was me."

Zach's eyebrows knit together. "I know it's none of my business, but what was this other person like?"

Though my instincts urged me not to divulge such information to a complete stranger, I smiled and said, "Mind if we sit down?"

We did, at one of the small tables for two.

Then I realized the gravity of what I'd done, and my eyes shifted to my backpack as I considered making a run for it. But I glanced up, and Zach sat there, his hazel eyes ablaze with curiosity, and he looked so much like the Zach who'd saved my life that I *couldn't* just walk away. So I took a deep breath, and began. "He was just like you. And when I say just like you, I mean it." I looked up from my latte and at Zach, whose eyes were fixed upon me. "He…" I sighed. "He was *you*. He looked exactly like you, acted exactly like you…" here I started to tear up, calling the *real* Zach to mind. I stared into my latte, trying to hide my looming tears.

Zach (not the Zach *I'd* known) spoke up. "You said you thought you'd never see—the other me I guess.."—here he chuckled at this odd sounding set of words—"What did you mean by that?"

"How can I explain this without mentioning Vitreusia?" I wondered silently.

"Well," I choked, "He—he died…"

Zach's face was now awash with a mixture of shock and bewilderment. "What happened?"

"No, Leigh," I told myself, sternly, mutely. *"Don't tell him—you can't trust him!"*

but I found myself saying, "I could've been shot—but he jumped in front of me, and, and—he got shot, instead." I replayed the incident in my head. I could see Zach running over to me. *"I will defend you to the end, Leigh."*

I just managed to restrain a sob, and Zach

inquired, "Didn't he go to the hospital?"

I nodded. "They did all they could…but he..he didn't make it."

Zach's eyes were starting to water now. "Did you get to say goodbye?"

I took a deep breath. "Not..not really. He said one last thing to me before he was rushed away by all the doctors…"

"I don't mean to pry," Zach started, "but I'm quite interested in the doings of my..my other self…what were those last words?"

"Don't, Leigh. You can't trust him with this information. stop, Leigh! **stop!**" I scolded myself, but the words—Zach's last words, which had propelled me to fulfill my destiny as Vitreusia's hero, spilled out of my mouth. "Be strong, Leigh. Be strong for me."

No sooner had the last word of the second sentence left my lips than Zach froze. For almost a whole minute, he didn't move—he didn't even blink or breathe. I got up from my seat to get help, but then Zach began to move and breathe again. His eyes seemed clearer somehow, and he fixated them upon me. Slowly, he got up from his seat. "Leigh?" he asked, the single word sounding so heavy that I expected it to hit the floor with a clatter.

My heart felt as if it would burst. "Zach…" I breathed, rushing over to my friend and throwing my arms around him in a tight embrace. "I can't believe it.." I sobbed as we held onto each other, both of us afraid to let go.

"Neither can I, Leigh," murmured Zach.

"Neither can I."

IV.

Slowly, I unwrapped my arms from around him and stepped back. Looking into Zach's hazel eyes, I asked, "Why didn't you recognize me before?"

"I had no memory of anything that happened in Vitreusia," replied Zach. "As far as all that went, my mind was a blank slate."

I threw my arms around him again. "I don't know how your memory came back…but I'm so glad it did."

"So am I," answered Zach as he returned the hug. "I find it astonishing that I could ever forget or even be compelled to forget someone like you."

I looked up at him, a twinkle in my blue eyes. "I assure you that I would've taken your memory to my grave—even if I never saw you again."

He smiled. "To be honest, I am baffled as to why we *are* seeing each other again."

"Austin never said anything about what happens to non Vitreusians who die in Vitreusia…neither did Christina."

Zach was silent for a few minutes, evidently thinking something over. "Well, given the nature of

Vitreusia when it's not in utter turmoil, I'd say that very few if any 'mortals' have died there."

I nodded. "So what you're saying is that there haven't been many occurrences of this…incident."

"Exactly, and the less often such things occur, the less is known about them. If rain was a rare thing, it likely would have taken scientists a good deal longer to discover what caused it. This is not much different."

"If it's so rare for a mortal to die in Vitreusia, then we may never know exactly *what* happened in your case."

"We might not," Zach agreed. "Interactions between worlds are tricky."

I rolled my eyes. "Well duh."

Zach just smiled. "Speaking of such things, I assume that you defeated the enemy and then chose to return to Earth when the question was asked?"

"Yes, I just managed to get the better of Darren."

I told Zach all about what had happened in Vitreusia since his death, beginning with when the doctor broke the news to me and ending with when I chose to go back to 'Terra'. He listened intently, and never once interrupted my narrative. When I had finished he shook his head, saying, "I should've seen that one coming with Austin and Christina. They've always played off of each other so nicely."

Then my cell phone rang. I flashed an embarrassed smile at Zach and answered it (it was my Mom calling). "Hello?"

"Leigh, where are you, honey?" asked Mom, her voice unusually sweet.

"What's going on?" I wondered as I replied, "Just at that little café on the corner of main street, Mom. Thought I'd grab a latte and do my homework." Well, at least all of *that* was true…I wasn't about to enlighten her as to what had happened at the café (again, any explanation would either sound crazy or mention Vitreusia—or even *both*.).

"Okay, sweetie. How much longer do you plan on staying, dear?"

I raised an eyebrow at the accolades that were flowing from the other end of the phone call. "Um…ten…fifteen minutes, I think?"

"Okay, darling. See you soon." And she hung up. I slipped my phone back into the front pocket of my jeans.

My facial features must have revealed my puzzlement, for Zach questioned, "What's wrong, Leigh?"

"Oh, uh, my mom just called. Just wanted to know where I was and everything."

"Hmm. Is there more to this than you're divulging to me at the moment?"

"Well..yes, I mean, it's probably nothing, but my mom was acting a little-over-the-top nice, you know?"

Zach nodded. "I get what you mean. It's probably nothing—maybe she's just having a really good day."

"Yeah," I agreed. "Maybe she's forgotten about

yesterday already."

Zach raised an eyebrow. "Yesterday?"

"Mhmm, she was getting a little suspicious and worried after I lifted the couch so easily…and then, *of course*, I had to be glowing when she came into my room that night."

Zach's face turned ashen. "Your powers?! She saw you glowing?"

He grabbed my hands, squeezing them hard. "Leigh, look at me. Has anyone else seen any—er—suspect behavior of yours?"

"Well…" I then gave him the details of the school day and what had gone on in Mr. Bonnell, Miss Hogan, and Mr. Elwood's classes. With each tale, Zach's features grew more worried and anxious. When I finished, he took a deep breath, and said, his voice trembling, "Leigh, you are in great danger."

"Wh-" I began, but Zach cut me off.

"We need to get out of here—quickly. Grab your backpack. Hurry."

Just as Zach had spoken the last word, a man came through the door and spoke to one of the employees at the counter.

The auburn-haired girl nodded, and then raised her voice to say, "is there a Leigh Kline on the premises?"

Zach's features were grim. "We're too late," he said, in a voice so quiet I could barely hear him.

V.

My heart began to beat wildly once more. "What do we do?" I whispered to Zach frantically. He pressed his lips together and put his hand to his forehead. I waited, my breathing becoming quick and shallow. Finally, a sad expression came over Zach's face.

"There is nothing we can do at the moment. You will have to go with them."

Horror took over my face. "Can't you help me?"

"Leigh, listen. There is nothing for you to do now but to give yourself up. I give you my word that I will not abandon you...now go."

I swallowed hard and walked up to the front counter. "My name is Leigh Kline," I said, doing my best to hide the fact that I was absolutely petrified. Almost immediately, half a dozen police officers rushed into the building. I was taken aback. "What's wrong?" I asked, my voice shaking.

"Come with us," one of them said. "You need to be tested right away."

"Tested?" I repeated in disbelief. "Tested for what?!?" Just then, my mom came in. She looked like she'd been crying.

"Oh, Leigh…" she sighed. "I can't believe you'd do this."

"Do what, Mom?" I asked, utterly confused.

The policeman closest to me shook his head sadly. "She's denying everything."

"Denying *what?*" I half shouted, half screamed. "What is going on here?"

"You're going to come with us, miss," said a policeman sternly, his green eyes serious.

"Come *where?*" was my anguished answer. Again, I received no response to my query.

As they led me out the door of the café, I threw a distressed glance towards Zach, who looked extremely frightened. *"For himself or for me?"* I wondered as I got into the back of the police car.

"Where are you taking me?" I asked.

"The police station," replied the driver shortly.

I could feel the color drain from my face. "Why?"

He only sighed and shook his head sadly in response, and I grew more alarmed.

By the time we'd arrived at the police station, I could barely walk in, my knees were knocking about so badly. "Sit down in this chair," an officer said as we walked into a plain, barely furnished room. I did.

One policeman sat down across from me and

said, "Now, when did you start abusing substances?"

Fear and rage rose up simultaneously in my throat, choking my words as I responded, "What are you talking about?? I've never done that in my whole entire life!!! I would never even *think* of doing such a thing!!" I cried, close to tears between all the anxiety and fear.

The policeman was unmoved, and he stared at me coldly with his blue eyes. "The sooner you come clean the better it will go over," he said plainly.

"But I haven't done anything!" I shrieked.

"Then you will allow us to take a sample of your blood."

I pounded my fist on the table as I replied, "Gladly! The sooner I'm out of here the better!"

"The test results are overnight, so you will have to stay either here or remain under house arrest during that time."

"*What!*"

The officer did not respond but got up and left the room, motioning for me to follow him. My mom was waiting outside, her blue eyes restless, her expression troubled. I rushed to her at once.

"I haven't done what you think, Mom, you'll see. They'll test me and everything will be clear."

She looked at me with a visage full of doubt that cut straight to my heart. "I haven't done anything," I whispered again.

It was decided, after the nurse from the lab had taken my blood sample, that I would remain under house arrest until the test results came in. I got into the car, and Mom looked ahead—as if I wasn't even there, and I knew she was really mad with me now. She always ignored me like that when she was especially furious about something I'd done. This time, though, I had done nothing.

I leaned back against the seat and closed my eyes. Everything would be alright tomorrow. The results would come in, and they'd find out I wasn't on drugs after all. Hopefully the extreme trepidation that Zach had expressed in the café was without meaning. I had a premonition, though, that his alarm was not insignificant.

I hardly slept at all that night—I could not stop thinking to myself, *what is going to happen to me?*

It was a question such that I both desperately wanted and dreaded the answer.

VI.

The next morning, I awoke to the doorbell ringing. My curiosity getting the better of me, I crept down the hallway and hid in the coat closet. I peered through the crack to see who was here. It was a police officer. "The test results are in," he said. I was barely able to prevent myself from letting out a big sigh of relief. He put a sheet of paper down on the table. "It's even worse than we thought," he said.

I almost fainted away into the mess of jackets and raincoats behind me. *Worse than they thought!!* How could that be!?! My heart pounding like a drum inside my chest, I listened to the police officer say, "no traces of drugs or medication of any sort were found…but her blood is highly unusual—there are no records of such an incident like the one we are dealing with." My mom's face was the definition of astonishment. "Mrs. Kline," said the police officer, his face grim. "We are dealing with something much more serious than a simple case of substance abuse. I think we will have to call in the CIA or the FBI—perhaps both." My heart was in my throat. The <u>FBI?</u> The <u>CIA?</u>

Just then my phone vibrated, and I just about jumped through the ceiling, it scared me so badly. I pulled out my phone. I had a new text from a phone number that I didn't recognize. It said: "Leigh, it's Zach. Is everything okay??"

"Zach.." I stopped holding my breath, feeling a short blip of relief. I replied:

"Right now, yes, I guess so…but there's a policeman here right now and he said that they're probably going to call in the CIA or the FBI!!" I slipped my phone back into the pocket of my jeans (I'd slept in my clothes last night) and went back to eavesdropping. "Does she *have* to go to this research facility? Phenomenon or not, she's still my daughter and I do *not* want her to be taken all the way to some top-secret investigation center in D.C.!" I gasped for air. They wanted to take me to a *research facility!?!* In *Washington, D.C.?!?*

My phone vibrated again, and I whipped it out of my pocket. It was Zach's reply. "This is not good…it's exactly what I was afraid of in the café yesterday."

My hands shaking, I texted him back: "Now the officer is saying that they're going to take me to a research center in D.C.!!"

Zach's response came not a minute later. "Don't go, Leigh!! Hide somehow or run away!! Once you go into that place you'll never come back out!!"

Panic started to set in as I typed my reply: "There's nowhere I can hide and if I run someone will see me right away—I have nowhere to go and no friends who would help me no questions asked.."
I sent the message and heard the officer saying to my Mom: "I'm notifying the FBI. Your daughter will go to the research center in a few days."

"You can't just *take* her!" Mom shrieked.

"Ma'am," said the policeman calmly. "She is dangerous."

"No she is not!!" protested Mom indignantly. "She is a sweet girl and she'd never hurt anyone!"

"I believe you Ma'am, I believe you," answered the officer in a calm, steady voice. "But we cannot be sure of exactly what we are dealing with here. The best possible solution at this point is to call in the FBI and see what we are up against. I will let you know when the agents are on their way. Good day, Mrs. Kline." And he got up from the table and left.

Mom stared after him, looking to be on the verge of fainting, but she regained her composure and grabbed the home phone. I knew at once that she was calling my dad. "Lawrence?" she half squeaked, half whispered. "Please come home right away. Yes, it's about Leigh. No dear, something worse than that. *Please come home quickly!*" and she hung up.

My phone vibrated again. It was (of course) Zach. "I…don't know what to do, Leigh." I nearly cried. Zach…my fearless, selfless friend Zach was at a loss of what to do.

I snuck back into my room and began playing Candy Crush on my phone, pretending that I'd been there the whole time. I'd just gotten settled when Mom practically burst into the room. "Leigh, what is going on?" she demanded.

"What do you mean, Mom?" I asked as innocently as possible.

"You know what I mean, Leigh! The glowing, the strength, the inhumanly quick reflexes!! What has happened to you? *Tell me!*" The only option that presented itself to me was to remain silent.

The front door slammed, and my mom flew out of my room. It was my dad. From my bed, I could hear my mom's voice, raised in anguish as she poured out the story of the morning. I ventured out of my room only once in the two or so hours that my parents discussed the situation—and by 'venture' I mean grabbing a granola bar and an apple and rushing back to my room. Then my heart jumped into my throat. The doorbell had rung.

I could hear the sound of my mom opening the door, and a woman's voice saying, "Juliana Forester, agent for the federal bureau of investigation." *The FBI! They were here already!!*

In desperation, I sent another text to Zach: "The FBI—they're here!" Footsteps neared my room, and my heart beat so fast I feared it would give out. Trembling all over now, I sent one last message.

"Help me, Zach!!"

VII.

Another footfall reached my ears, and I whirled, my face the very picture of terror. Imagine my surprise at setting my eyes upon not some Amazon woman, dressed in black with dark sunglasses, but a petite lady with black, wavy hair, olive skin, and caramel-colored eyes. She wore designer jeans and a bright orange blouse. She *did* have a pair of sunglasses, rhinestone studded with white frames, but those were atop her mass of black hair. "Are you Leigh?" she asked, smiling warmly.

"Yes…" I answered cautiously.

"Lovely meeting you, Leigh," she said, extending a small, smooth hand.

I grasped it and shook firmly, the way my dad had taught me to. "Nice to meet you, too," I said, forcing a smile and faking enthusiasm.

"I'm Juliana Forester, but you can just call me Juliana. No need to bother with the Ms."

"Okay…Juliana," I said, wondering what question she'd ask me first.

"I hear you have some supernatural powers, huh?" said Juliana in a casual sort of way as she clipped her sunglasses onto her sleeve. "Extreme strength and unusually quick reflexes? I also hear that you glow at random intervals as well. Your white blood cell count is also quite high…"

"How do you know all of this?" I asked, my eyes narrow.

"Ah, so it *is* true!" said Juliana triumphantly.

Oh, no!

This Juliana looked sweet and harmless enough, but she definitely wasn't as clueless as she looked. "Do you have any idea how you obtained these powers, Leigh?" she inquired in a voice that seemed overly sweet (or maybe that was just her natural tone—I hadn't heard her speak any other way yet). I sure wasn't going to divulge that information, so I gave her a blank stare. "Leigh, my friend, I asked you a question." I gritted my teeth at those words—"my friend."

"If you were really my 'friend', you'd get up, leave the room, and tell all your buddies in the government to leave me alone," I thought to myself.

"There is no answer to that question," I lied.

"Come on, Leigh, just tell me. It'll be our little secret," said Juliana, staring into my eyes and smiling pleasantly. I sighed. Maybe I *should* just tell her—if she wouldn't tell anyone else, how could it hurt? I got ready to spill the beans—and then my phone vibrated twice. I had a new text. Startled, I jumped a bit and looked to see who it was from. *Zach.*

"Whatever happens, Leigh, don't ever tell them about Vitreusia—doing so would put all Vitreusians in great danger!!"

As soon as I read the text I deleted it. If they confiscated my phone later on, that was not something I wanted them to see. I looked up, and Juliana was eyeing me curiously. "Friend of yours?" she asked.

I smiled feebly. "Yeah."

"So, are you going to tell me how you obtained these special abilities of yours, Leigh, or will we have to figure it out?" It took all my self-control to hide my nervousness.

"Listen, I'm just as puzzled as anyone else!" I protested, throwing my hands up in the air.

Juliana reached out and patted me on the arm. "Don't get upset, Leigh," she said calmly. "We'll have this all sorted out soon enough. My partner Jonah is talking to your parents right now, and hopefully he can convince them to give us permission to remove you to the research center."

*Oh, **no!** The research center!* That was the absolute last place that I wanted to go!! Zach's text came to mind. *"Once you go into that place you'll never come back out!!"* I heard a footstep, and I jumped. A man stood in the doorway. He was of average height and was very muscular, with sandy brown hair and grey eyes. "Juliana." He motioned to her with one of his large hands. They whispered earnestly for about thirty seconds, and then he left. Juliana came back into the room, a grin on her pretty face.

"Your parents have agreed to have you transported to the research facility. Only the country's most brilliant scientists are permitted to work there, and they'll have you figured out in no time. We'll have a first-class flight arranged for tomorrow morning. See you soon, Leigh."

Putting her sunglasses back on the top of her head, she left the room. I buried my head in my hands, panic setting in. I texted Zach, a tear dropping onto the screen. "They're taking me to the research center tomorrow." I returned to my previous position. Two minutes later, my phone made the chiming noise again.

Zach had replied. "Oh, Leigh...I wish this were as simple as just throwing myself in front of you." I swallowed hard, a lump rising in my throat.

"Me too, Zach," I whispered to myself. "Me too."

VIII.

Dinner was extremely quiet, and less than five sentences were spoken during the meal. When we were finished, the cleanup was spent in silence as well. I grabbed my homework and half-did it (who knew if I would ever go back to school again?) until about nine, and then Dad said that I should get to bed ("your flight leaves at quarter to eight"). I closed my book and said goodnight to both of my parents, giving them tight hugs.

When I'd been lying in bed for awhile, my phone buzzed, startling me out of the drowsiness that had slowly wrapped around me like a warm blanket. It was another new text from Zach. "When does your flight leave?" To which I replied:

"At a quarter to eight tomorrow morning."

A few minutes later his answer lit up the screen. "So soon?!"

"The FBI convinced my parents that the sooner

I get to the research facility, the better."

"Well isn't that just great."

"You're telling me," I replied almost immediately.

Zach's next response puzzled me. "Hey…" *"Hey what?"* I wondered, and the question was soon answered with another text from Zach. "You should go back to Vitreusia and get Austin and Christina's opinion on this."

"You think so?" was my rejoinder. Just two minutes later my phone vibrated once more and I read the answer:

"Definitely."

"K leaving in five minutes," I responded, then deleted the last few messages, double-checking that my phone was still on vibrate.

I put on my jeans and a striped t-shirt, quickly running a brush through my hair. Grabbing the dagger out of my pajama drawer, I put my phone in my pocket and strode over to the mirror with the golden border that had started all of this. Pressing my hand upon the glass, I softly chanted, "Aperite vitreus ostium nam Terram istam ego sum amicus.." The glass swiftly melted away before my eyes, and standing on the other side of the mirror was Sabrina, her navy hair pulled back into a braid. "Welcome back, Leigh," she said as I stepped into the void, her pink eyes gleaming excitedly. As the image of my new room was swallowed up by the blackness, Sabrina took my hand and led me through the darkness.

Stopping suddenly, she chanted in a soft voice that was nearly a whisper, and a rectangular door appeared, light flooding through as it swung open. No sooner had the two of us crossed the threshold than the darkness which had enveloped us vanished, and I was looking down upon Vitreusia once more. This time, however, there were no blazing buildings, no screams of horror, no cries for help.
"Everything's back to normal again," Sabrina murmured as she gazed upon the peaceful scene.

"Thanks to you, Leigh—and Zach too, of course."

"Thank you, Sabrina."

She nodded. "Let's go. I know where Austin and Christina are."

"Lead the way," I responded. And she did. Our ten-minute journey ended at an unfamiliar house.

"This is Austin's home," said Sabrina in reply to my bewildered look.

She knocked twice and said, "You have a visitor!"

I heard footsteps and voices within, and the door was opened by Christina, whose purple eyes sparkled at the sight of me. "It's very good to see you, Leigh!" she exclaimed, embracing me. Moments later Austin was at the door as well.

"Leigh!" he said as he shook my hand heartily. "What a pleasant surprise." Sabrina left, waving a silent farewell to the three of us.

"Austin, Christina, I have to talk to you," I stated.

"Let's get started, then," answered Austin cheerfully, leading Christina and I to his family room.

When we were all seated, I stole a glance at both Austin and Christina's foreheads. Their gashes were in the process of scabbing over, and I assumed that the wounds on Austin's forearms were doing so as well.

With a deep breath I began, "Are you guys ready for a *huge* shock?" Austin and Christina exchanged a quick look.

"Fire away, Leigh," said Austin.

"Okay.." I answered, and told them of Zach's baffling restoration, from the very beginning when I realized he was speaking at my school, and I finished off the account with the astonishing happenings at the café.

"I don't know exactly what's happened here," I concluded, "but it's something extraordinary." Christina's porcelain features were pale, and Austin's green eyes looked as if they might fall right out of their sockets.

After a few minutes of sitting in silence with his azure eyebrows knit close together, Austin spoke. "There is nothing—absolutely nothing in the history of Vitreusia that is even remotely like this."

"Incredible." murmured Christina.

"To be sure," I answered. "but I also have something else to discuss with the two of you, of a very serious matter."

"Do begin," said Austin.

I related the occurrences at school, the ordeal at

the café, the accusations of substance abuse and what the test actually *did* reveal—and concluded with the events of the day. When I was done talking, they both looked extremely disturbed, in the exact same way that Zach had in the café.

Christina walked over to me and put her arm around my shoulder. "Leigh," she began, "you may need to reconsider your choice to stay on Earth—because not only are you putting yourself in danger, you're putting all of us here in Vitreusia in danger. Suppose you are coerced—or forced—to reveal the cause of your superpowers?"

"I would not—nor will I ever," I asserted firmly.

"Leigh," said Austin kindly, "I know you wouldn't. but these people are desperate for answers. There's no telling what they'd do for them."

"Listen, Leigh," said Christina in her soft yet firm way. "I advise you—and I'm sure Austin agrees—to seriously consider staying here, where you are safe, and no scientists will study you, nor any agents question you."

Austin nodded. "Christina is right, per usual." To which comment Christina rolled her purple eyes (but I could tell by her smile she was appreciative of Austin's compliment). I glanced from one Vitreusian to the other.

Swallowing hard, I said, choking up as I did so, "I've already been forced to leave the state and city that I love—must I also say goodbye to my entire *world?*" Silence claimed control of the room, and I could tell by the looks on my friends' faces that they were at a loss for words.

IX.

I looked from Christina to Austin and back again, tears beginning to sting my eyes. "Leigh," began Christina, but I interrupted her, overwhelmed by my strong emotions.

"I thought you told me that I'd never be sad again, Christina!" Lowering my voice, I said, "I guess you were wrong—because these certainly are not tears of *joy!*"

Feeling a pang of guilt for my outburst, I didn't dare look up at either one of them.

Then I felt Christina's hand on my shoulder. "You're right, Leigh," she said. "I did tell you that, and I was wrong—very wrong. I'm sorry, Leigh. I never expected half of Vitreusia to be ablaze when we returned, either."

"Look," began Austin, "we can't keep focusing on what the past should have been or what we thought it would be. We have to concentrate on the present and what can be done with the future." He paused for a moment and then said, "Do you *want* to go back, Leigh?"

"I do, but I don't," I replied.

"Explain yourself," Austin implored me, and Christina seconded him with a nod.

"Well, staying here *would* be nice and all, but then there's my family, my friends, and Zach…the latter would be able to visit every week or so, but I'll only be allowed to see the formers one more time—maybe never again."

Austin sighed. "If you really want to, you can return to Earth. I warn you, though, to do so would be to risk your life—and all the lives which you went to such great costs to save."

"Not a single word will escape my lips," I promised them both.

Austin took a deep breath. "Well, let's take you back."

Soon the three of us were in the void, and I hugged Christina and shook Austin's hand before they began to chant, and the blackness swallowed them up completely.

The next thing I knew, I was being shaken awake by my dad. "Get up, Leigh. The FBI will be here to pick you up in a little more than an hour." At the sound of *that* sentence, my blue eyes opened wide. "I have a list of what you should pack on the dresser." he said, leaving the room. I walked over to the dresser and surveyed the list. If you just looked at the list, and that alone, you'd think I was going on vacation for a week. However, the research center was definitely *not* a vacation, and unlike a vacation, I had no idea when I'd be back.

My suitcase stuffed to bursting, I headed downstairs. Mom was reading the paper, and I could hear Dad's razor buzzing. "There's cereal in the cupboard." Mom said from behind her paper. I silently walked over and pulled out the granola. I poured myself a big bowl and sat down at the table (I hate the taste of milk in my cereal). I had just put away the bowl when the doorbell rang. *The FBI.*

Moments later, Juliana walked in, her hot pink high heels clicking on the linoleum floor. Her hair was pulled back into a perfect ponytail, which swung around in a rather annoying fashion when she walked. "Good morning, Leigh!" she trilled (yes, this ridiculously sweet, high voice was indeed her natural one). "Good morning, Mr. and Mrs. Kline!" It took all my self-control not to roll my eyes and snap, "shut up, will you?" "Are you ready, Leigh?" she asked, turning to me. I shrugged.

"Yeah, sure, I'm ready to get locked up in a research center. Sure," I thought to myself.

Juliana turned to my parents. "Shall we go?" she asked.

They got up, and we got into Juliana's red Ford escape without a word being said. The drive to the airport was short, sweet, and extremely awkward.

We pulled into a parking spot right next to a huge Chevrolet truck. "Leigh, you can get out now," Juliana said (man, her voice was grating on me).

"Jonah and Agent Denniston will take you on the flight to Washington, D.C." I got out, as did my parents. My dad lifted my suitcase out of the trunk for me and then gave me a hug, as did my mom.

"We'll be there a few hours after you, Leigh," she said, stroking my hair. "Be safe and listen to the agents. Alright?"

"Alright," I mumbled.

They got back into the car, and Juliana drove away, maneuvering the car with ease. The doors to the truck opened, and Jonah got out of the driver's side. Then from around the back of the car came a woman whom I presumed was Agent Denniston.

One look at her, and a chill of fear permeated my heart. Firstly, she was extremely tall—at least six feet tall, if not taller. Secondly, she wasn't all dolled up like Juliana had been in her designer jeans and cute blouses. Instead, she wore black jeans and a black fleece, and had purple tennis shoes on her feet (the only color besides black she wore). She had no sunglasses that I could see (perhaps they were in her little clutch purse, which was black, of course), and that made her all the more frightening, as her steel-blue eyes looked as if they could freeze a pot full of boiling water. Her brown, chestnut-highlighted hair seemed to be either curly or wavy (it was hard to tell when she had it in a tight ponytail).

"You must be Leigh Kline," she said, with only a tinge of politeness, no more, no less. I nodded, struck speechless by this intimidating figure. "Well!" she half said, half barked. "Let's go."

Walking alongside the two of them, I decided to try and make a run for it. I did not like the looks of Agent Denniston one single bit. I ran, as fast as I possibly could. I did not know where I was going— just away from Agent Denniston. That was all I wanted to do.

Although I was a decent sprinter, I was no match for Agent Denniston's long stride and breakneck speed (did this woman run sprints on a daily basis??). She closed in on me and tackled me, pinning me to the ground. "Ouch!" I cried as she twisted my arms behind me (great Scott, was she *strong!*).

"Get up," she snapped. And I did. Jonah gave her a warning look, and she let go of my arms. "No more games, Kline," she ordered, staring into my eyes. I looked away from her laser beam gaze. "Got it?" she asked.

"Yes," I said meekly, "I've got it."

She turned away from me with a noise like a snarl, and Jonah gave me a sympathetic look. Evidently Agent Denniston wasn't very popular among the FBI agents (not that I'd be surprised to learn of *that*).

We breezed through customs and security, and awhile later we were boarding the plane headed to D.C. Jonah was next to me (he had the window seat), and Agent Denniston was across the aisle. I could feel her blue eyes boring into me as the plane lifted off the runway. I hardly dared to move under her bulldog-like watch. I remembered the look of utter panic upon Zach's features when the police took me out of the café, and I understood it completely—completely too late. *"How am I going to get out of this mess?"* I wondered. Then a horrible thought occurred to me. ***Maybe you won't, Leigh.***

X.

The drive to the research center was slightly less uncomfortable than the plane ride (mostly because Agent Denniston was driving and not staring holes through my brain). After twenty minutes of complete and total silence, Agent Denniston pulled into a medium-sized parking lot, saying as she did so, "We're here."

I studied the building with bated breath. It resembled a high school, possessing that cardboard-boxish look that both public and private schools alike commonly have. Big capital letters proclaimed: 'Ronald Reagan Research Center'. I couldn't help wondering if the person who came up with the name for the building had known what would take place inside it.

I didn't have much time to ponder that, however, because Agent Denniston had pulled into a parking spot. "Let's go, Kline," she said, yanking the keys out of the ignition. I unbuckled and got out. Jonah still sat in the passenger seat, and I kind of felt sorry for him. "You too, Harris!" snapped Agent Denniston. Jonah was out of the car in half a second flat. "Grab her luggage while I check in," she ordered, stalking off towards the entrance of the building. Jonah nodded and opened the trunk.

"Geez," he muttered as he put my suitcase down on the pavement. "She's a trip, that Agent Denniston," he said with a wink.

I smiled weakly. "A bit bossy, though, isn't she?" I asked in a sarcastic tone.

"Ha!" scoffed Jonah. "That, and she's as ill-tempered as a drill sergeant who's had one meal and two hours of sleep."

"That about describes her," I agreed.

"Don't tell her I said that, though," Jonah said, glancing towards the building.

"Trust me, I won't," I assured him, calling the incident at the airport to mind. "I don't want to get tackled again." "She played rugby in high school and college—oh brother, here she comes!" said Jonah, indicating a tall figure dressed in black emerging from the building.

I might have been mistaken, but I thought I heard Jonah swear under his breath as Agent Denniston approached. "We're all clear," she said, her blue eyes roving from me to Jonah and back again. "Take Kline to her chambers. I have some work to do."

"Got it," Jonah answered quickly.

Agent Denniston's eyes narrowed. "What was that, Harris?"

Jonah cleared his throat. "Right away, Agent Denniston."

"Thank you," She said, although the tone of voice in which those words were said would have been more appropriate for "I hate you."

She got into the car and drove off, her expression one of grim determination. "Wonder where she's off to next," remarked Jonah as we watched her turn out of the parking lot. "To be honest, as long as it's somewhere that I'm not I don't really care."

"No love lost, eh?" I asked with a teasing grin. Jonah scoffed.

"As warm and friendly as an iceberg, and just as endearing," he commented as he scanned his badge to get in. "Follow me." And I did, down long, white hallways with lots of white doors that had white doorknobs…we turned left and right, but each hallway looked exactly like the last.

Finally, Jonah stopped in front of a door and pressed his thumb into the middle of the doorknob. The knob made a clicking sound, and the door opened just a crack. "After you, Leigh," Jonah said, standing aside. I walked into what looked like a suite in a five star hotel. It was that nice.

I could see a nicely furnished sitting area, with a flat screen TV. There were two other doors, and upon opening them, I saw that they led to a bathroom and a bedroom. The singular thing, however, was that *everything* was white. The walls, the carpet, the sofa..it was *all* blindingly white. I turned to Jonah, who was ready to leave (the fact that he had his hand on the doorknob could not be ignored). "What's with the white in this place?" I asked him.

He shrugged. "Honestly, I really don't know. It kind of grates on me. Well, I've got to go. I've been assigned another mission already, and I think Miss Congeniality might be my partner again." Here he let out a long sigh. Juliana was 'nice', but I wondered what she was really up to. Agent Denniston was, to say the least, frightening and very irritable. Jonah, though…he at least *acted* like a normal person (whether he was or not, I figured time would tell).

I was kind of sad to see him go. "Well," I said, "Good luck with *that*."

He grimaced. "Thanks," he said. "I'll surely need it. Perhaps I'll see you around, Leigh." And he was gone. I was now alone in the all-white room. Out of curiosity, I tried to turn the doorknob. Sure enough, it wouldn't budge. Correction. I was *locked in* the all-white room. Alone.

XI.

"Don't panic." I told myself. *"Stay calm."* That, of course, was extremely difficult to do, considering the circumstances. To keep myself occupied, I unpacked all my things, organizing them carefully.

I had just closed the dresser drawer when I heard a knock at the door. "Hello?" said a woman's voice. My breathing grew shallow. *"Now what?"* I wondered as I emerged from the bedroom.

I came face to face with a woman, who was probably in her late twenties or early thirties. She had blonde hair cut in a bob and striking green eyes. She was (of course) wearing a white lab coat, and what looked like a blue button-up shirt underneath it (possibly the first splash of color that I'd seen in this strange place). "Good afternoon," she said, giving me a tight smile. I then noticed that there were some purplish rings under her eyes, indicating that she hadn't gotten enough sleep lately. "You must be Leigh Kline." I nodded (I wasn't fond of how everyone automatically knew my name). She proffered a hand about the size of mine, with long nails that had a flawless French manicure.

"I'm Claire Erikkson."

"It's nice to meet you," I said as we shook hands.

"It's my job to figure you out," she asserted, looking me in the eye.

A chill ran down my spine, but I was able to cover up my apprehension with a smile (yet again I was thankful for being an amateur actress).

"Are you a doctor?" I asked.

She nodded as she set a bag of equipment on the family room side table. "Yes, and a scientist as well."

"What's your area of expertise?" I inquired.

"Oh.." she smiled modestly. "Well, I suppose I'm at my best in biology, but I'm quite experienced in chemistry and medical science as well." Chemistry…medical science…all this was vaguely familiar to me.

Then I remembered why. "Didn't you win the Nobel Peace Prize a few years ago?"

Claire looked slightly startled at my question, but then recovered her poise. "Why, yes, I did."

Juliana wasn't lying when she said that only the country's most brilliant scientists work here," I thought to myself.

"Shall we do a couple of simple examinations, Leigh?" queried Claire, rifling through her cloth bag. *"That sounds like trouble,"* I thought, but then figured it was best to acquiesce to her request (after all, the last thing I needed was to arouse more suspicion). The exams began.

She tested my eyes and my hearing, my reflexes…every time I thought we were done with the questioning and probing, she'd pull another strange instrument out of her bag (so I mentally dubbed her Mary Poppins).

At long last, she was finished (and her beat-up blue notebook had three or four new pages of notes). "Well, Leigh," she said as she gathered up her tools, needles and so on and so forth, "I guess that's all for now. I'll be back *very* soon. Have a good evening." With that she gracefully swept out of the door. *Click*.

I was alone again. I turned on the TV and clicked through the channels subconsciously. A sharp rap made me jump, and Juliana came into the room, accompanied by my mom and dad. I got up to greet them, and I noticed that my parents' faces looked rather worried and grim. A split second later, though, they both smiled as if nothing was wrong. "Are you alright, Leigh?" my mom asked.

"Um, yeah..I'm fine. All the white is a little annoying, though."

Juliana laughed. "I know, right? This place needs a pop of color!"

"It sure does," I agreed.

When I looked at my parents, they were again acting off. Their eyes were fixed on Juliana, and I thought I saw distrust and fear lingering in my mom's blue eyes and my dad's brown ones. Again, I only caught a glimpse before the intimation was covered up once more.

I showed my parents around the place, and then they stayed for a little while—twenty minutes or so.

When my dad had finished telling his latest tale (he traveled often for his job and always had an interesting anecdote to recount), Juliana stood up.

"Well," she said, "we'd best be going."

My parents stood up at once. "Yes, Leigh, we'd better go," my mom concurred.

Juliana held the door, and as mom left, following dad, she turned and made eye contact with me. Her blue eyes flashed as if she were trying desperately to communicate something. Then she looked away and went out the door. Juliana, with a broad smile and a cheesy wave that made me clench my teeth, pranced out into the all-white hallway.

As I sat in the white armchair, I turned the visit over and over in my mind, trying to figure out what all those queer looks I was getting from my parents were about. All of the sudden, my phone started to ring, startling me out of my deep thought. *My mom's cell.* Quickly I answered.

"Hello?"

"Leigh!"

"Mom?"

"Honey, I'm so sorry!"

"Mom, what?" I asked, puzzled.

"I never would have done this to you, dear, but we didn't have a choice…"

My heart rate went through the roof. "Mom, *what*

do you mean?"

"Juliana—" she began, but was suddenly cut off. *"Mom? Hello?"*

I heard a sound like the click of someone with a handset phone hanging up, and then a female, computerized voice. "Unauthorized communication. Violation of inmate code of conduct number thirty, paragraphs H, I, and J. Connection terminated." Then there was only a dial tone to be heard.

As I hung up the phone, my hand shaking, I had a sinking feeling that there was something more sinister behind all this than either Zach or I had ever imagined.

XII.

It took awhile for me to gather up enough courage to move from where I sat in the white chair in the white room. I kept telling myself to be brave like I had been in Vitreusia, that it would all be okay, that I'd get out of this place somehow. In spite of my efforts, my breaths came shallow and fast, and my hands shook like leaves. That was because, first of all, I was *alone*. Secondly, I was definitely, absolutely *trapped* in this room. And third: Somehow I knew, deep down inside, that some of these agents were worse than Darren.

Given that third thought, it is understandable, then, that when Jonah came through the white door I had to bite my lip, pinch my cheeks and cross my eyes just to keep from completely freaking out. This, of course, looked, at the very least, eccentric, and at the very best, amusing. but Jonah's reaction threw me for a loop. His grey eyes opened wide in an expression

118

that could only be fear, and he rushed over to where I was in the chair, exclaiming, "Leigh! What have they done to you?!"

At once my hands flew down from my face, my eyes straightened out.

I looked at him through frightened blue eyes and said, "Nothing…yet."

He breathed a sigh of relief. "Forgive me for my outburst, Leigh. I just returned from my mission with Agent Denniston, and I was immediately sent to check on you. I guess my imagination got the better of me."

"Imagination, indeed," I mused. This, his reaction to my appearance upon entering the room, was a clue. I tucked the event carefully into the back of my mind, to reflect upon later. While I did this, I replied to Jonah's apology.

"Do you want me to forgive that outburst, or would you rather I forget it?"

Jonah looked startled. "Leigh, why do you ask?" My temper threatened to explode at this response (he knew darn well *why!*), but I was able to rein it in for the time being. "I don't know what's going on here, but I do know that it's not anything good. Seeing as a little thing we'll call *my life* could be hanging in the balance, I want to figure it out as quickly as possible."

Jonah quickly strode over and sat on the (need I mention it was white) couch and faced me, looking me in the eye. "Leigh," he began, "I'm not entirely sure of what is happening in this operation myself. The one thing that I do know is that this research center is anything but what it's cracked up to be." That, coming from someone who was supposedly on the inside of this process, was very unsettling.

Tucking that, too, into my mind for later, I said, "That isn't all you know, is it?"

Jonah looked around, as if to make sure there was no one else in the room. He pulled a strange device out of his pocket and flipped a switch on it.

"I might as well tell you now," he said. "but you mustn't interrupt me or ask any questions, because I—we don't have very much time, perhaps a minute before our favorite agent breaks down the door." I would have stammered, "What?" but he had asked me not to talk, so I held back. "That agent I was partnered up with on the last assignment? Juliana? She's one of **their** chief members of the staff. She knows almost *everything* about this project. And this is the procedure that nearly eighty-five percent of *all* the agents don't know anything about! Only a select few of us—Agent Denniston and I, for example, know that this research center even exists! And she and I were talking a little bit about what we *do* know about this—and that's pretty much nothing. We're almost totally in the dark as far as this. I've asked Juliana, but her lip-glossed lips are sealed. I—" here he glanced towards the door, where shouting could be heard outside.

Whatever or whoever it was, they were approaching rapidly. "I don't have time to tell you how Juliana acted before," he said, "but I didn't like what I saw at all." He pressed the strange device into my hand. "That disables the cameras and microphones in the room," he explained. "Just don't use it too often." I was barely able to nod, shocked by what I had just been told. Just before he exited the room, he said, "I'll do my best to figure this out, Leigh."

I had one quick look into his grey eyes before he went out the door, and the sight immediately began to haunt me. I hadn't seen calm, cool knowledge or even a hint of understanding. No. What I *had* seen was the unmistakable expression of a person who was both hunted and haunted. Only moments later I could hear Jonah's plea, "I was only following orders and checking in on her!" I looked at the small, black device in my hand. Quickly I went into the bedroom and put it in the pocket of my jeans, flipping off the switch as I did so.

Then I grabbed a book and sat down in the armchair. Seconds later Agent Denniston burst into the room. "*What* is going on in here?" she barked. Just before the door closed, I saw Jonah being led away by a couple of agents I hadn't seen before. *Cover for me*, he mouthed. I swallowed hard. I put down my book and stood up, facing Agent Denniston head on.

XIII.

Agent Denniston did not take her steely blue eyes off of me for a second as she asked me, "What was Harris doing in here?"

"He was just following orders, Agent Denniston, and coming in to check on me." I could tell by her grim expression that she didn't buy it.

"He also talked to you for a while, did he not?"

"Yes, he did."

"About what?"

Doing my best to keep track of what the camera overseers had seen and heard, I replied, "Well, first he apologized for acting strange when he came into the room, and then I asked him if he'd rather I forget or forgive...then I asked what was *really* going on here, because I wanted to know, and he just gave me a roundabout answer. And that was all."

"What about the last question you asked him?" I decided to play dumb.

"What last question?" I inquired.

Agent Denniston whipped out her cell phone and tapped on it a few times. Suddenly I heard my own voice saying, "That isn't all you know, is it?" I'd never been the swearing type, but hearing *that* made me want to use a couple of colorful metaphors.

"That question," said Agent Denniston triumphantly. "Oh, and right after that question was asked, Harris looked around furtively and pulled a strange device from his pocket. Immediately after he had done that, both the cameras and microphones planted in your room went blank."

At once I plastered a look of fake shock upon my face. "You've been *spying* on me?!?"

Agent Denniston's face took on an almost guilty look. "Never mind that. What was the mechanism Harris produced from his pocket?"

"I don't know," I replied quickly. "It might have been a two-way radio or something, because of how your cameras turned off. I think my question had made him nervous and he just pulled it out to avoid answering me."

"What about the cautious glances he made around the room before he got the gadget out of his pocket?"

"There was some noise outside the door, and he was slightly startled by it, and at first didn't know where it had come from," I answered.

"Harris is a highly skilled and heavily trained

agent. Do you really expect me to believe that he was startled by a trifling noise outside the door?"

I was becoming frustrated, first of all with Agent Denniston's habit of calling people by their last names, and secondly, her ruthless line of questioning.

"Well, first of all, Agent Denniston," I began vehemently, "His name is Jonah, *not* Harris. Secondly, he had been made nervous when I had asked my question—probably because he was hiding something from me, like every single one of you in this *whole entire building,* and **that's** why he was so easily startled."

"Well!" huffed Agent Denniston as she walked briskly towards the door. "Headquarters will certainly be disappointed by the lack of news!"

And with a slam of the white door she was gone. I breathed a sigh of relief. *"That was easier than I expected,"* I thought to myself. *"It was almost too easy."* I dismissed the thought. Agent Denniston had obviously been satisfied with my explanation of things, or she wouldn't have left the room. but what if she wasn't? What if she had left to get backup of some sort, perhaps from another agent—maybe two? I wrote off that possibility as well. If she had wanted backup, she would've used one of her many gadgets or possibly even a secret signal.

I came to the conclusion that I had fooled her—for now. When I checked the time, I realized it was getting into the evening—eight o' clock. By the time I showered and changed into my pajamas, it was eight thirty. I crawled into bed, worn out by the events of the day. I read a couple pages of my book, and then my eyelids became so heavy that I put it down and drifted off.

I awoke to a knock. "Leigh, it's Claire. May I come in?" I laughed to myself at the irony of such a question as I got out of bed and changed.

"Come in," I called, brushing my black hair. And she did. She was carrying the same bag which she'd used yesterday. She set it down on the white coffee table.

"I have to ask you some questions," she said.

"*Oh, no,*" I thought. "*She's going to try and wring something out of me the way Juliana did.*"

"The test results are extremely unusual," she began. "Do you have any idea why that could be? Have you started or stopped taking any supplements or medication?"

"No, I haven't," I answered.

Claire (she was Mary Poppins in my head now) wrote in her notebook briefly, then asked, "Have you been around any unusual or rare substances or minerals or a combination of them? Have you been experimenting with chemicals of any sort? Have you recently been exposed to radiation of any kind?"

"No, no, and no," I answered. Claire's thin eyebrows knit together.

"How strange," she remarked as she wrote in her notebook. I remained silent, watching her with a mixture of apprehension and curiosity.

She flipped through her notebook, reading each page thoroughly. I waited with bated breath. Finally she closed the notebook and looked me in the eye. "Leigh," she began, "This may sound crazy, but I've examined my notes with the utmost attention to detail, and this is the only feasible hypothesis for your strange abilities. Leigh, have you experienced any supernatural or otherworldly phenomenons recently?"

I resisted the urge to gasp, knowing that I would give myself away. "No," I replied decisively, making sure that my voice was steady and I looked Claire in the eye. Claire looked at me inquiringly, and I knew at once that she doubted my answer. "I may be wrong…" she said slowly, "but I always triple-check my work for correctness and scientific accuracy. However, there is always the off-chance that I have made a mistake."

She reached into the pocket of her lab coat and pulled out a phone. Apparently it could also function as a walkie-talkie, because she spoke into it, saying, "Doctor Erikkson requesting Doctor Benedict Fulton to report to suite seventy-four in hallway eleven, repeat, suite seventy-four in hallway eleven, over."

Almost immediately a deep voice responded, "This is Doctor Fulton. I will be there in three minutes or less. Over."

"Copy that," Claire replied. "Over and out." She pocketed her gadget and turned to me. "Doctor Benedict Fulton is another brilliant scientist here at the research center. Whenever I need a second opinion on any case to make sure I have theorized correctly, I utilize his experience and knowledge." Soon the door opened, and Doctor Fulton came in.

He was a tall, slender man with a shock of white hair and knowing brown eyes. His face, although quite wrinkled, had a kindly look. "Doctor Erikkson," he said, shaking hands with her. "It is a pleasure to assist you again." Then he turned to me. "And you must be Leigh." I nodded. He shook my hand firmly. "It's very nice to meet you, young lady. Now I can finally put a face to the girl who has the most gifted scientists in the country scratching their heads!" I gave an inept laugh.

Doctor Fulton then asked Claire, "what would you like me to do?" At once she opened up her notebook.

"I would like for you to perform these tests on her," she said, moving her pencil down the page of notes, "and see if you get the same results and come to the same conclusion that I did."

Doctor Fulton put on a pair of reading glasses and studied the page intently. "Indeed."

He ran through the same procedure that Claire had not twenty-four hours ago, in his quick, efficient way. Then he gathered up his equipment. "I will have a verdict for you in a couple of hours, Doctor," he said as he left the room.

Moments later Claire also departed. "A clarification is at our fingertips," she remarked as she went out the door. With a sigh I returned to my book. Several times I considered texting Zach, but the conversation I'd had with my mom yesterday haunted me too much. As a matter of fact, I hadn't touched my phone since. I was pretty sure it was bugged in some way, just like the room I was in.

I had just finished my lunch (which was brought in to me on a *white* tray with *white* utensils) when the door opened, and who should come in but Juliana. Her black hair was twisted into a perfect bun, and she wore an orange blouse and white jeans. "Hello, Leigh!" she said cheerily, her caramel eyes sparkling.

"Hi, Juliana," I answered vacuously, picking a piece of lint off my t-shirt. "May I ask you a question?" she inquired in her annoyingly sweet voice.

"I guess."

"You know that the doctors and scientists who work here are only trying to help you, don't you, Leigh?"

"Do I?" Juliana's smile faded slightly, and I continued, "Do I know that they're, quote, 'trying to help me', presumably so I can lead a normal life? Do I? Well, if you want the answer, the answer is no. Because I don't know precisely what is going on here, what every agent and doctor and scientist is hiding from me."

Juliana opened her mouth, about to respond, but I cut in before a word could come out of her mouth. "Don't try to tell me you're not hiding anything. It would be a waste of your time. I won't believe a single word you say."

A quick flash of temper shone through Juliana's eyes, but it was gone in an instant.

"Calm down, Leigh," she said sweetly. "I only want you to tell the doctors and scientists the truth."

"Ah, I see," I replied bitterly. "You don't want

me to lie, but it's okay for you to do it."

"You *are* lying, then!" cried Juliana in a fit of passion.

"I never said I was! I only said that *you don't want me to!*" I retorted.

"Listen, Leigh," Juliana began (she had somehow regained control of herself). "You *must* tell the doctors all you know. The more they know, the sooner they can pinpoint what the issue is. And the sooner that happens, the sooner you will be allowed to leave."

My eyes narrowed. "Is that a threat?" A glint of ire appeared in Juliana's eyes, and the smile was wiped from her face. She glared at me, her olive-skinned hand on the doorknob.

"You *will* tell the truth," she said darkly before she closed the door behind her.

XIV.

I was alone for a few minutes, my heart pounding wildly. Claire came back into the room, and I eyed her suspiciously.

"Juliana said you had something else to tell me."

"Oh, she did, did she?" I thought to myself. Then I had an idea—an idea that would probably get me into more trouble—but at this point, I didn't care all that much. I nodded slowly, avoiding eye contact with Claire.

"And?" she prompted.

"Don't try to figure me out. You can't do it, and neither can I."

Anger splashed across Claire's face. "I'm a doctor and a scientist with three degrees, multiple awards, and a Nobel Peace Prize. I *can* figure you out. Just watch me!"

The door slammed, and she was gone. I picked

up my book again, and was not surprised one bit when ten minutes later the door flew open and Juliana stormed in. "You!" She cried furiously. I did my best to look startled and innocent.

"What?" I asked.

"Have you forgotten what I just told you not even twenty minutes ago?" she exclaimed.

"I told you, I'm not holding anything back."

"Ha!" Juliana scoffed. "Why should I believe you?"

After a moment's thought, I answered, "that's a good point. Why should *I* believe *you?*"

Juliana's face was grim. "Because you don't have a choice," she said briskly as she marched out of the door.

For the next twenty or twenty-five minutes, I was left alone. I read a chapter of my book and debated whether I should risk trying to contact Zach. He had no idea where I was, or if I was even still alive. But my phone was, in all likelihood, bugged, and if I contacted him that could lead to trouble for him.

The door opened, making me jump. *"Who is it now?"* I wondered. I was shocked to see that it was Jonah, and behind him was a tall figure in a lab coat. "How are you, Leigh?" he asked concernedly.

"All right for now," I answered.

"I've brought someone with me," he said, gesturing to the stranger that stood behind him. I eyed the man cautiously. His hair was mostly covered by a ball cap, which was maroon colored and had the logo of the Washington Redskins on it. The color of his eyes was difficult to make out from where I sat, but I figured them to be hazel. "This is Doctor David Jones. He wants to ask you a few questions." At the word *questions* I was turned off, and my blue eyes flashed petulantly as Doctor Jones produced a clipboard and seated himself on the sofa.

"Well," he said in a gruff voice, "First off, would you mind giving me your hand?"

With an inward sigh I did as he asked. Doctor Jones took my hand in his and gave it a quick squeeze. The feeling of that gesture gave me déjà vu. I knew that I'd felt that same exact hand squeeze before, but the details of when and where escaped me...then as I remembered, my heart skipped a beat. *Zach had always squeezed my hand in the very same way.*

Hope lit me up from the inside out as I looked "Doctor Jones" in the eye. but my hope was short lived, for Doctor Jones' face was far too wrinkled and aged to be the visage of my loyal friend.

After asking me a couple more questions, Doctor Jones said as he looked over Claire's notes, "Well, Leigh, I think I have a solution for you. You'll need to pack up everything in this room, though. How quickly can you do that?"

"Umm..five minutes?"

"Good," he replied. "Agent Harris and I will wait right here." I packed everything at lightning speed.

"Done!" I announced, coming out of the bedroom. Immediately the two of them got up and headed towards the door. "Where are we going?" I asked.

Doctor Jones turned around. "Shh! Keep your voice down and follow us." So I did. Quickly, efficiently, Jonah weaved through the maze of white, Doctor Jones and I following.

When we turned a corner, I saw the same doors that I had entered this building through just a few days ago. *"What's going on here?"* I wondered as we approached them. Jonah swiped his card, and Doctor Jones and I went out of the building, Jonah holding the door for us. Doctor Jones took the lead, and Jonah fell into the rear. Doctor Jones produced some car keys and unlocked a blue car about twenty feet away from us.

When we got to it he opened the trunk. "Here, give me your suitcase," he said. I looked at Jonah, my eyes asking him a hundred questions at once. He nodded, as if to say "listen to him." I handed him my single suitcase, and he put it into the trunk and closed it. Then he walked over to Jonah and shook his hand firmly.

"Thank you so much for all your help, Agent Harris."

"My pleasure," Jonah replied.

"Miss Kline, please get in the car," Doctor Jones said, walking around to the driver's side.

"Go, Leigh. Do as he says," Jonah prompted, his gray eyes serious.

"but..why?" I thought but didn't say as I opened the car door and slid into the leather seat. Doctor Jones started the car, and was going to pull out when Jonah knocked on my window.

"Wait!" he said. "I forgot to give you something." I rolled down the window, and he handed me two credit cards. "Use these for any expenses," he said. I looked at him questioningly, one eyebrow raised. "Good luck," he said, and Doctor Jones pulled out of the parking space.

As Doctor Jones drove and the research center's brick exterior began to fade into the distance, I looked at the credit cards that Jonah had given me. On one, the raised name was Carly Piszczek. On the other, the name stated was Andrew Kleman. I turned to Doctor Jones at a red light and questioned, "Why did Jonah tell us to use these cards if the names on them are not ours?"

"I see there is no fooling you, Miss Kline," Doctor Jones said, unbuckling his seatbelt and removing his lab coat. He buckled himself in again, took off the baseball cap and, reaching for a water bottle in the cup holder, poured some water onto a few napkins which were stashed in another cup holder and rubbed his face with them. As he rubbed the water-soaked napkins on his face, the wrinkles and lines vanished completely. Then he looked me in the eye. "Do you recognize me now?" he asked, smiling warmly. I was astonished.

"Zach!"

He nodded, crumpling up the napkins, putting his seatbelt back on and taking hold of the steering wheel once more.

"Jonah helped me," he said as he flipped on his blinker. "He sought me out. Said he'd read the texts that you and I exchanged. He told me where the research center was and helped me get in. And as for the disguise, I was a makeup artist for plays in high school." I was quiet for a little while as I thought everything over.

"What about these credit cards?"

"Oh, yes, those," Zach said. "The names on those cards are *our* names from now on."

I gasped. "What do you mean?"

Zach took a deep breath. "What I mean is that we are going to have the FBI, CIA, and every police officer in the entire United States searching for the two of us. We have to assume different names, or otherwise we'll get caught immediately. Start memorizing your name now, and don't *ever* call me Zach unless we are in this car. Got it?"

I swallowed hard. "Yes."

For a few moments silence permeated the vehicle. "Where are we going?" I asked.

Zach took a deep breath. "Well…first we have to get out of D.C. That's the most important part. Our final destination is, I hope, Libby, Montana."

"Libby?" I repeated. "Montana?"

"Yes," Zach replied. "It's remote and pretty much unheard of. Hopefully no one will find us there—at least not for awhile."

He was quiet while he switched lanes, then spoke up again. "Another thing, Leigh. When we stay in a hotel tonight—and any other time we stay at a hotel, we're not taking any chances of being recognized. You're going to go in first, while I stay in the car.

You'll get a room and go up to it. I'll come in twenty minutes later and get my own room. Before we check in, I'll tell you when I'm going to check out. You'll come down twenty minutes later, check out, and then meet me in the car. Okay?" I nodded. Then Zach looked in the rearview mirror. "Oh, no," he said in an undertone.

Quickly I looked in the rearview mirror also, and saw a black truck. Zach switched lanes, and so did the black truck. When he sped up, it did, too. "We've got an agent on our tail already," Zach said through gritted teeth. "Hang on while I try to shake him." He swerved into an exit and then made a quick right-hand turn. *The truck was caught at the light!* Then he entered a mall plaza and came out the other side, heading towards the highway once more. When the truck and its driver did not reappear behind us, he wiped away the beads of sweat that were beginning to form on his forehead. "I wonder what will get to me first-the agents or the stress," he remarked.

"Hopefully neither," I said, already worried about him.

Zach sighed. "Yes…hopefully."

XV.

For the next few hours, Zach and I talked. We started off with my experience at the research center, and then we moved on to other subjects. I told him about my parents (whom he'd never met), my extended family…and he, in turn, told me about his.

He was adopted, he said—under very strange circumstances, which had not been disclosed to him until his eighteenth birthday. His adoptive parents said they'd waited until his eighteenth birthday to tell him the story because it was unusual and somewhat troubling. They narrated, word for word, what the nurse who worked in the maternity ward had recounted to them.

Because the story was so unique, Zach had them recount it once more, and wrote it down. He read it almost every day, and so memorized the account. And he began: "Leigh, you're going to be the first that I tell this story to. I've kept it to myself for a long, long time. My parents, that nurse and a few others are the only ones who know about it. My siblings know a few of the most important parts, but they are not aware of all the details."

"Zach," I said, "if this story is so personal that even your own siblings are in the dark as to some of the particulars, don't feel like you have to relate it to me."

"No," he replied. "I want to. Especially since I don't know how much time we have left together…now more than ever."

I massaged my forehead. "*Please*, Zach. *Please* don't talk like that."

He sighed. "Sorry, Leigh. It's the truth, though." Memories of his death in Vitreusia began to assault me, and I did everything I could to push them away.

"You were saying?"

Zach took a deep breath. "Before I begin, I have to remind you that the story is told from the nurse's point of view. I'm going to tell it from beginning to end, and you can ask me questions—if you have any—when I'm finished. Okay?"

"Okay," I answered.

Zach cleared his throat and began: "It was about ten thirty at night when they came in—a young, handsome couple. The man was tall and strong, the woman small and dainty. The man's hair was a bright yellow that stood out in the dimly lit room. The woman had straight, light brown hair. The man carried the woman in his arms. She was pregnant and obviously in labor. "Please help my wife!" the man pleaded in a voice overcome with anguish.

I, along with some other nurses, grabbed a stretcher and helped the man place her on it. We wheeled her to a room where for ninety minutes she was in hard labor. At last, the baby came out. He was nearly two months premature, and was immediately rushed to the NICU. Both the parents begged the doctors not to take the baby away, but to no avail. They did not seem to understand that their son must be taken away from them temporarily if there was any chance for his life.

I stayed with the doctor and helped stabilize the mother, which took a good twenty-five minutes. Then the two of us had to leave momentarily, to check on the condition of the baby and a few other patients, as we were quite understaffed that night. 'Can you watch over her for a little while?' I asked the man. He nodded, and we left the room.

As it was, no one was free to check on them until a full half hour had passed, and my friend Gina was sent to check on the enigmatic couple. Less than five minutes later, a startled shriek echoed through the second floor. I was on that floor at the time and came running to see what the matter was. Gina's complexion was pale, her expression shocked. I took her shaking hand in mine. 'What's wrong?' I asked. I looked into the room. *The couple had vanished.*

The hospital bed where the woman had lain was empty; the sheets being pulled all the way back, touching the floor.

The room was a shambles—not one thing was as we had left it. The lights in the tiny bathroom were turned on—and nothing in there was amiss, save that the bar of soap which had been on the countertop of the small vanity was now on the floor.

Together we rang the front desk and asked that the police be called at once. The room was taped off and an alarm went out for the young couple. Weeks of exhaustive searching brought nothing to light, and after over a month of investigation, the authorities gave up."

Zach turned to me (we had been caught in slow-moving traffic for twenty minutes now) and said, "I would've been placed in a foster home once I was released from the hospital, but that nurse said she knew a couple from her church who had fertility problems and would adopt the child in a heartbeat. Those are the people I know as my parents now."

I was stunned speechless by the fantastic story, and it was a good minute or two before I spoke.

"Wow…I really don't know what to say to that, Zach. 'I'm sorry' doesn't sound right, because you have parents, if not your biological ones, and, technically speaking, your birth parents *could* still be out there. All I can say is…*wow*. Just…*wow*."

Zach smiled wanly. "That was my response to the tale as well, Leigh. I'd known I was adopted since I was twelve, but I never knew that it—my adoption—was surrounded by such intrigue. I often wonder what happened to my biological parents—not that my adoptive ones aren't good enough for me, because they're great—but because when one has that much vagueness about one's birth, well, it's impossible not to theorize about it."

The traffic moved faster now, as we were passing the scene of the accident which had caused the jam. "Maybe one day I'll find out what happened to them," Zach said as he pressed his foot on the gas pedal, "but right now, I've got a more important job to do—keep you safe."

XVI.

It was completely dark when we pulled into the parking lot of a Comfort Inn. Zach parked the car as far away from the entrance as possible. "Well, I'll see you in the morning, Leigh," said Zach before I got out.

"Okay. Good night," I responded.

I got out of the car and headed in. The woman at the front desk eyed me skeptically, as if she wondered why a young person like me would be traveling alone, but the only thing she said when she handed me my room card was "Have a nice stay." I thanked her and headed for the elevator.

The room was a far cry from the all-white one at the research center, but it was clean and besides, it wasn't like I was staying long anyway. I showered, changed and crawled into bed. Physically, I was very tired, but mentally, not so much. The events of the day were replaying themselves endlessly in my head.

I tossed and turned, unable to make my mind relax. After an hour of lying in bed, hovering between sleep and wakefulness, I drifted off. The first thing I saw when my eyes blinked open was a gun, and, holding the gun, Agent Denniston. "Thought you could get away, eh, Kline?" she snarled. "Think again. Now get out of bed."

I had no choice but to comply. She snapped handcuffs onto my wrists and marched me out of the room. I searched frantically for Zach. Had he been caught too? And if not, then what would he do when he waited for me to join him in the car—and I never came?

As I was led into the lobby, I gasped in horror. Zach was handcuffed, and a burly agent stood close by with a pistol. "We've got them both," Agent Denniston snapped. "Let's go." Zach was pushed into a red SUV, I into an orange Jeep. *I'm sorry*, Zach mouthed as the tinted glass window closed.

My heart beating wildly, I looked at Agent Denniston, who was starting the car. "Where are we going?" I managed to say.

She laughed, a short, hoarse bark of a laugh. "Well, Kline, *you* are going back to the research center. And your friend? He'll spend at least ten years in jail."

"*No!*" I cried. Then it all vanished before my eyes. I was still in the hotel room. It was seven fifty-eight am. Zach would be checking out at about ten after eight. I had to get going.

My heart still pounding from the horrid nightmare, I got dressed and packed up all my things. I took the elevator to the lobby and ate breakfast, checking my watch after every few bites to see how much time I had until I was supposed to check out.

Fortunately, I checked out without any difficulties, and met Zach in the car. "You look pale," he remarked upon my getting in.

"I had an awful dream," I responded.

"About...?"

"The FBI catching up with us."

"Ah," he responded, "No wonder you're pale."

"How much more distance do we have to cover?" I asked concernedly.

Zach gave a short, nervous laugh. "Oh, only thirty-four hours' worth of driving—about two thousand miles."

"We've got a long way to go," I commented.

Zach shook his head. "Much too long of a way, I'm afraid," he replied, and I silently agreed. Two thousand miles was a long way, and the list of things that could go wrong was pretty much endless, from relatively small matters like a flat tire to the absolute worst scenario (getting arrested by the police or the FBI). To say the least, our chances of making it to Libby looked slimmer than a photo-shopped swimsuit model.

The car was quiet for awhile, and then Zach said, "Leigh, this is kind of random, but isn't there some kind of chant to get into Vitreusia?"

"Uh...yeah," I replied.

"Could you teach it to me? If you know it, that is."

"Sure," I answered, and for a short amount of time my troubles (and his) were forgotten as I taught him the chant.

Neither of us were exactly American Idol material, so we both had quite a few laughs over our singing voices (or lack of them).

Then, when Zach had it down, I questioned, "Do you think we should just go back to Vitreusia? Is that why you asked me to teach you the chant?"

Zach took a deep breath. "Well, yes and no. I hope we'll be able to make it to Libby…but just in case something goes wrong…well, I want the two of us to be prepared."

I gulped. "What is it, Leigh?" Zach inquired.

"Nothing," I muttered, quickly looking out the window.

"Something," Zach insisted. "Don't think you can fool me, because you can't. What's bothering you?"

I inhaled shakily. "I…I don't want to lose you again, Zach. Once was hard enough."

"Slow down, Leigh," Zach said firmly. "You're getting ahead of yourself. When I said *in case something goes wrong* I didn't necessarily mean something of those proportions. Let's say an agent catches up with us, and you pass out in all the excitement. I will need to know the chant to escape for the time being, correct?" I nodded. "I can think of several other situations that are not as severe as you fear they will

145

be, but where my knowing the chant is vital. In other words, Leigh, *relax*. Panicking will make things worse, even if they weren't very bad to begin with. Okay?"

He turned his full attention to the road. "And, Leigh," he began again after a few minutes' silence, "I would take an arrow—or something else—for you again without hesitation." I choked back tears, for images of Zach's death in Vitreusia had begun to come to mind yet again. "However," he continued, "that is the very last resort, only to be fallen back upon when there is no alternative. I don't want to be killed any more than you do—but if that's the only way to keep you out of harm's way...then so be it."

I swallowed hard, keeping the tears at bay. "Thank you, Zach. I'd do the same for you—if I were brave enough."

Zach scoffed as he switched lanes. "Leigh, you were courageous enough to fight—and defeat—the man who tried to kill you, killed me and captured two other friends of yours. I don't doubt your heroism— and neither should you." I didn't answer, as I couldn't think of a suitable response, and by the time I did, I was alone in another mediocre hotel room. The rejoinder was this:

"Yes, I was brave enough...but only because of your own bravery. Without you, I don't think either of us would be where we are right now."

I crept under the covers, breathing a sigh of relief that no one had caught up with us yet. I hoped our luck would hold out until we made it to Libby...and with that thought I fell asleep.

The next morning I showered, dressed and headed for the lobby—not unlike the morning before. However, when I headed for the desk to check out, twenty minutes after Zach said he would check out— there he was, at the front desk! I covered up my emotions and nonchalantly walked towards the front desk, as if I had never seen him before in my life.

When he left, I checked out. I made small talk with the blonde girl behind the desk so that Zach had plenty of time to get in the car and start it. When I sat down in the passenger seat, I felt very relieved that even though our plan for checking out didn't exactly go as planned this time, we had emerged unscathed. Hopefully the employees didn't suspect a thing.

We were getting back on the highway when I noticed that a blue convertible was trailing us closely. It was so close behind us I could see the driver, a serious man in a t-shirt. "Zach?" I began cautiously.

"Yes?" he inquired, shifting his eyes from the road to me and back again.

"I think someone's following us."

He glanced in the rearview mirror and grimaced. "Hang on, Leigh," he commanded me.

He sped up, and the speedometer jumped from sixty-five mph to seventy-five. Then he braked—hard and suddenly, and we flew forwards, our seatbelts locking and nearly taking our breath away. He swerved into an exit and made a sharp right turn at the light. "The highway is far too dangerous," he remarked as he turned onto a side street. "We'll have to take lesser-known routes. It will be safer, but unfortunately, it will take longer, too." Repressing a sigh, I looked out my window, and who should be in the lane next to us but *Agent Denniston*, riding a black motorcycle!

XVII.

Quickly I looked away. "Zach! Zach!" I said.

"What?"

"Look—over there! Another agent…one of the worst ones, too!"

Zach glanced over at her and softly swore, making me gasp. *"Don't* comment on it—I'm the one doing the stunt driving!"

I smiled a little, then stole another peek at Agent Denniston.

She wasn't wearing a helmet, and her chestnut ponytail swayed violently. One look at her pursed lips, knit eyebrows, and stern blue eyes told me that she was on a mission. I swallowed hard and turned back towards Zach. "What will we do?" I asked.

"We have to get by her somehow," he answered.

He put his blinker on and turned onto another side road. "Recalculating," said the GPS (which Zach had me hook up as soon as we got off the highway). I looked into the rearview mirror.

"I don't see her."

Zach checked as well. "Neither do I. I think we've managed to lose her."

I set my lips in a straight line. "That was too easy. She's got to still be following us." Zach and I peeked into the mirrors several more times, but saw no sign of her. I actually managed to *relax* for a few hours.

As the sun sank below the horizon, I glanced into the rearview mirror just as we stopped at a red light. There was a red car pulled up close behind us, and in the driver's seat—*no, it was impossible*—but there she was, rhinestone studded sunglasses and all. *Juliana!* "Uh..Zach?" I began, quite uncertainly. "Would you mutilate me if I told you that there is an agent following us again?"

He immediately glanced into the mirror and sighed heavily. "I would never do that, Leigh—not on purpose."

I was puzzled. "Huh?"

"Have you seen the way I have to drive to get away from these people?" he questioned.

"Oh."

"Well, hang on 'cause here we go *again*."

He slammed on the brakes and made a wild right turn. The speedometer went up to eighty. "Recalculating," said the GPS.

"She's still there!" I informed him. Zach's face

was serious as he swerved into the *wrong lane,* and put both feet on the brake pedal. We stopped with a jerk, and Juliana went speeding past. Zach made a U-turn.

"Recalculating," said the GPS. Zach ignored it as he made a risky left turn.

"I see her car!" I told him.

"Does she see us?" he asked.

"I don't know…"

Then she made a reckless left turn and began to swerve through traffic. Horns honked, and drivers yelled in indignation. "Yeah, she still sees us!"

Zach did not respond but turned into a Kohl's parking lot and drove through it at forty miles per hour. We came out on the other side and he swung a right turn. "Recalculating," said the GPS.

"Oh, shut up," Zach retorted.

"Warning. Speed limit reduction ahead," the GPS admonished.

A minute later, we whizzed by a school speed limit sign (at fifty miles per hour now). Juliana was far behind, but Zach didn't take any chances. He braked slowly this time and turned into the school parking lot. Quickly he drove behind the school.

"I hope this works," he said.

"Recalculating," said the GPS.

"Oh, brother," Zach said in exasperation.

After ten minutes there was no sign of Juliana. Zach exhaled in relief as he turned out of the parking lot. "We finally lost her," he said. As we pulled into the hotel parking lot, I sighed, becoming at ease once more. But when I stole a glance at Zach, he did not look like he was free from worry. Rather, his facial features were pinched and tense as he parked the car. "Goodnight, Leigh," he told me, trying to cover up the uneasiness in his hazel eyes.

"Goodnight," I replied tentatively, for I had observed his anxiety. Knowing that Zach did not fret over trivial matters, his angst was rapidly rubbing off on me. Zach perceived this and, taking my hand, gave it a quick squeeze and smiled reassuringly. I returned the squeeze and smile and went to check in.

Safely checked in and in my room, I tossed and turned in my bed for what seemed like hours before my eyelids finally closed…and stayed that way.

When I got into the car, Zach still seemed distressed. "How did you sleep, Leigh?" he inquired, a glint of concern in his hazel eyes.

"Uh…okay. How about you?"

"I've slept better," he responded. "Leigh, before I start driving again, I want to give you something."

Here he reached into his pocket, and handed me a compact mirror. It was predominantly purple, with an outer edge of silver. It had an intricate design etched into the top. I studied it for a moment, then gave Zach a questioning look.

"That," he said, "is for you to use to get to Vitreusia in an emergency. Always keep it close by."

"But what about you?"

"I was just there last night, Leigh. I cannot return for two weeks."

The words were a sharp blow to my harassed emotions. *"Why, Zach?"* I exclaimed, on the verge of tears. *"Why would you do that?"*

Zach sighed. "Leigh, I can't exactly tell you why I made the choice to go to Vitreusia last night, and I certainly hope you don't end up having to find out for yourself. I'll explain everything to you once we're settled in Libby."

I wiped away a tear. "Okay." I reached for my seatbelt, but Zach grabbed my hand.

His hazel eyes met mine as he implored me, "Leigh, promise me you'll use that mirror if there's an emergency, even if that means leaving me behind."

I choked. "I…"

"Promise me, Leigh!" he appealed, his voice crammed with emotion.

I took a deep, shaky breath. "I promise, Zach."

"Thank you, Leigh," he murmured as he started the car.

"No," I replied. "Thank *you.*"

Most of the morning was silent, as the two of us were still tense from yesterday's affairs. Then, as we gradually stopped glancing into the rearview mirrors to check for FBI agents, we began to talk to each other again.

We bounced from subject to subject (we didn't stay on the subject of sports very long—it bored me), and the hours started to go by very quickly once we began discussing plays and acting. Zach being a makeup artist, and me being an actress (on a very small scale), we had plenty to talk about.

I was so absorbed in our conversation that I was surprised when Zach parked the car. I stopped in the middle of my sentence.

"I guess I have to check in, don't I?" I asked.

Zach smiled fondly. "I guess you do. Goodnight, Leigh." He gave my hand a squeeze. "See you in the morning."

"Okay, goodnight," was my rejoinder as I got out of the car.

I checked in and went up to my assigned room. Changed into my pajamas and under the covers, I went over the events of the day. It had actually been pretty good. The only stressful part about it was in the morning, when Zach gave me the compact mirror. I reached under the pillow, pulled it out, and looked at it. Its metallic finish glinted brightly in the light of the bedside lamp. *"I really hope I don't end up having to use this,"* I thought to myself. And with that, I turned the lamp off, closed my eyes, and drifted off.

XVIII.

I woke up, dressed, and repacked my suitcase. I grabbed a muffin and a banana for breakfast, and when I was finished I headed for the front desk. I was taken aback to see Zach, still standing at the front desk, apparently in the process of checking out. I knew just what to do—I got in line behind him, acting nonchalant, as if the person in front of me was a complete stranger.

Presently Zach said to the middle-aged woman at the desk: "Well, ma'am, I'll be going now. Have a good day." And he headed for the glass doors.

As he put his hand on the stainless steel handle, a woman with dark hair sprinted into view. Several men were following her at a distance of a few feet. She burst through the door, knocking Zach over. She and the men behind her grabbed pistols from the holsters that were at their sides. The woman brushed her black, frizzy hair away, revealing a familiar face—

155

Juliana! "Stand down, Leigh," she hissed through her impeccable white teeth. My hand flew to the dagger (which still was in its sheath at my side) as Zach got up off the floor and dashed over to me.

Juliana's facial expression was a mixture of confusion and amusement. "Who is this?" she inquired in her overly sweet tone of voice. Zach and I both gave her defiant stares. Juliana cocked her pistol with a light, airy laugh. "Whoever he is, he's rather clever—I'll admit that. but the game is up, my dears. Going quietly will help your situation a great deal."

As she said this, she and the four men who were with her (I assumed they were other FBI agents) started closing in on Zach and I. Juliana held her pistol at the ready, while the others merely kept their hands on theirs.

Juliana was face-to-face with Zach when he swiftly kicked her legs out from under her, and she fell down on the mahogany carpet. Two of the agents came at me, and I pushed one into the other and knocked them both out with the bell on the front desk. An agent rushed at Zach and was judo thrown across the lobby. Zach and I took on the one remaining agent together, Zach disarming him and I throwing a swift uppercut that made him fall down unconscious.

I grabbed a gun from one of the unconscious agents and tossed it to Zach, and then grabbed one for myself. "I wouldn't use those." said a familiar high voice.

I whirled around and glared at Juliana. "Why?" I

challenged.

"I won't tell," she replied. Slowly she got up, clutching her gun. "Don't make me do this," she cautioned.

"Don't make *me* do *this*," I retorted angrily, hiding my gun behind my back.

"Leigh," Zach cut in anxiously, "Easy."

Juliana laughed. "Always the peacemaker, eh?" Zach looked puzzled. "I know you," Juliana continued. "You're that anti-bullying speaker. Always calling for peaceful methods. That's what your policy is."

Zach's face flushed in a rush of emotion. "Not always. I call for *action*. Non-violent action that is still firm and stern!"

Juliana waved her hand dismissively. "Ah, well, no time to argue over that now." She cocked her gun. "Come with me." Zach aimed his pistol, ready to cock it. Juliana *tsk*ed in disapproval. "Not an option, dear friends. Now, I have an important mission to complete." Without warning, she lunged at us, and suddenly, all I saw was red, and only red.

Rage and anger washed over my brain and body, and I cocked the pistol, which was still hidden behind my back. *Click*. "Fingerprint required," a robotic voice said. Zach swung his weapon forward and cocked it. "Fingerprint required."

Juliana pulled back, aimed her gun at us, and smiled knowingly. "Put the guns down," she said, but Zach and I gripped them tightly.

Then, suddenly, Zach's gun morphed into a pair

of handcuffs, which clicked into place on his wrists. I attempted to bring the gun out from behind my back..but I was handcuffed as well! Juliana leered as she approached us slowly. Zach and I backed up, Zach sliding in front of me protectively. "One false move," she warned, "and I'll shoot. I've been on your trail too long to let you slip away from me now."

"Stay behind me, Leigh," Zach directed me.

"Zach," I said in an undertone, hoping Juliana didn't hear me, "I don't want to lose you again."

"Neither do I," he answered.

He and I backed up until my back hit the front desk, and Juliana smiled artificially and ran her fingers through her black, wavy hair.

"How are we going to do this, my friends? The way where nobody gets hurt—or the way where there may be casualties involved?"

"I'd prefer that no one gets hurt," Zach replied, "but Leigh and I are *not* going with you."

The smile faded quickly from Juliana's face. "You leave me no choice, then," she murmured threateningly as she cocked her pistol again.

"Agent Forester!" gasped a weak voice. "You know this is against protocol!"

It was one of the agents which Zach and I had knocked out minutes before. Juliana laughed, shaking her head slowly. "My job and my reputation are at risk—do you really think I *care* about protocol? Leigh Kline and Zach Johnston, come with me. *Now.*"

Zach's face was grim. He looked at me out of the corner of his eye, then whirled around, grabbing my dagger out of its sheath and cutting through my handcuffs. Juliana fired, and the dagger fell to the floor. *Clang!* Blood leaked from a wound in Zach's left arm.

My knees began to shake. "Zach," I whispered, "Just stop fighting. We'll get out of this some other way, some other time."

"No, Leigh," he responded. "They'll guard us so closely after this so that there *won't* be some other time." As he said this, he winced in pain. A lump the size of an avocado pit was forming in my throat.

"Please don't do this, Zach!" I begged quietly.

"You have a minute before I take drastic action." Juliana cut in. Then she said on her phone/walkie talkie, "Stand down. I've got everything under control."

He turned a mournful pair of hazel eyes on me. "Leigh, there is no other way out."

"We could run," I suggested.

"The building's surrounded," he replied. I looked and sure enough, agents stood all around outside. "Do you have your mirror?" he asked.

"In my pocket."

"Good." He grabbed my dagger off the floor. "Here," he said, handing it to me. I cut through his handcuffs, and he hugged me briefly.

Juliana's caramel eyes flashed. "I have waited long enough." *Bang!* Zach crumpled to the floor, and I stifled a scream.

"Leigh," he said weakly, "Go!" Tears welled up in my eyes, and I knew what I had to do.

I opened up the compact mirror and chanted, tears running down my face: "Aperite vitreus ostium nam Terram istam ego sum amicus…" The glass of the small mirror liquefied to black, and I experienced a strange feeling. I likened it to being sucked up by a vacuum, except without the noise. It didn't hurt, although squeezing through a small space like that should have.

Everything was black, and I knew I was in the void. I walked a couple of steps, and then I collapsed, feeling very weak and distressed. My eyes blurred with tears, and a glowing figure walked towards me…and I saw no more.

IXX.

When I regained consciousness, all I saw was white, and my face felt unusually damp and cool. I reached out from under what I presumed were blankets and put my hand on my face. Realizing that there was a washcloth on my face, I pulled it off and sat up in the metal bed, making it creak.

The walls of the room I was in were a bright, cheery yellow. Light shone in through the window on the opposite side of the room. *"Where am I?"* I wondered. This was certainly not my bedroom at home, and if I was back at the research center, the walls would (most likely) be white.

Slowly, cautiously, I began clearing out the cobwebs that had formed in my memory. Everything came rushing back at me. Juliana...the handcuffs...Zach...the compact mirror he'd given me...I remembered it all now. I peeled back the covers and debated whether I should get out of bed.

Just then, I heard footsteps, and Christina came in, a worried expression in her purple eyes. "Are you alright, Leigh?" I scanned myself, and saw a splotch of blood on my white blouse. Quickly I averted my eyes from the sight. I knew that the stain was not my own blood, but Zach's.

"I…I guess so," I answered slowly.

Christina motioned to someone standing in the doorway, and Austin came in. His face, too, was grim, and his vivid green eyes were serious. He bent down and whispered in Christina's ear, and she whispered back to him in response. Austin nodded and said a few more words to her in an undertone. He produced a piece of folded up paper from his shirt pocket and handed it to me. He left the room, but Christina stayed behind.

As I opened it up, I realized that it was torn off a hotel notepad, and I immediately knew who it was from. The tears gathering in my eyes already, I began to read:

"Leigh:

I sincerely hope that you do not have to read this letter by yourself, and that I will read it to you in Libby or Vitreusia. This letter is a precaution, you might say, in case worst comes to worst. I will assume, then, that something has happened to me, and I am no longer with you. After the third day of our impromptu road trip, I began to seriously doubt that we would make it to Libby, and, if and when we did, that we wouldn't even be able to stay there very long. In essence, I realized that in our present situation, there was a great deal of danger involved.

I knew (and I told you this) that if you were in danger I would do all I could to protect you, and, if doing so was the only way to save you, sacrifice my life for you.

*With this knowledge, I took steps to make sure that if the worst **did** happen, my sacrifice would not be in vain. I bought the compact mirror, which I hope I have presented to you. I also went to Vitreusia and gave Austin and Christina very specific instructions. Yes, I cut off for a period of time what in some cases may be my only escape, but I did it for your safety—and that of Vitreusia as well. I know that you do not want to lose me again, and, as I have told you, I do not want to lose you again, either. but Leigh, the time we have spent with each other over the past week or so—every second of it—was a gift, a mysterious gift which allowed me to cheat death and be with you once more.*

*What I'm trying to say is that every minute was a minute stolen, every hour was an hour extra. I know that this situation isn't ideal—but life, for the most part, doesn't work like that. Time has to catch up with me, Leigh, sooner or later. Please, don't shut yourself away and grieve my absence. Instead, smile—your smile is absolutely breathtaking. Laugh, because your laugh is a beautiful one. I'm not saying that it won't be hard, because it will be. I'm not saying that you won't have bad days, because you will. but I know that you **can** push through this. You're a strong person, Leigh, and once you start believing that, you'll be stronger than ever. I would **never** give up on you—so don't ever give up on yourself. Farewell, Leigh. I wish you all the best.*

> *Sincerely,*
> *Zach."*

I gently laid the letter upon my lap, and two tears

splashed down onto it.

"Are you going to be okay, Leigh?" asked Christina softly, making me jump. I had forgotten that she was in the room.

"Maybe…" I choked out. Christina's purple eyes searched my face for the truth, and I burst into tears. "I don't know, Christina!" I sobbed, then murmured quietly, "I don't have any answers for anything right now."

Christina made no response, and when I looked up, Austin was at her side. I fingered Zach's name, which was signed in impeccable cursive. "I have to go back.," I said suddenly.

Christina and Austin looked up, startled. "Don't you see? Zach could be in Juliana's clutches right now! I *have* to go back and save him!"

Austin shook his head slowly. "I would not spend your only visit so rashly."

"Wha—what do you mean?" I stammered.

Austin's face was solemn as he looked me in the eye. "Leigh, part of Zach's instructions to us were as soon as you came through to the void, to alter you so that you became a Vitreusian. As you know, a Vitreusian can only go to Ter—Earth once in their lifetime, for a time spanning less than twenty-four Earth hours. Attempting to do so again…is fatal."

"Why?" I asked. "Why did you listen to him? *Why did you do this to me?*"

Austin sighed. "Zach told us how the agents had halfway found you out. Our world is a vulnerable one, Leigh. If we know that it is in danger, we cannot stand by and do nothing about it. I *am* sorry, Leigh. But it was our duty."

"Wait for four and a half days, Leigh," Christina said. "Then two weeks will have passed on Earth, and Zach will be able to return."

"And if he doesn't show up, what will we do then?" I inquired.

Christina looked at me with anxious eyes. "I don't know, Leigh. I just don't know."

Four and a half days later...

As the sun set, Austin, Christina and I sipped punch on Christina's porch. The three of us were silent, and a feeling of gloom seemed to have washed over us. "He isn't here yet," I whispered. "They've probably imprisoned him in a room without any mirrors."

"Perhaps," Austin said quietly.

"I have to go back and save him," I said determinedly, setting my glass down.

"No, Leigh," Christina cut in.

"Why, Christina?" I demanded. "Why are you telling me to abandon my friend?"

"I'm not telling you to abandon your friend, Leigh," she answered, calmly and softly. "I'm only saying that it would not be wise to go back just yet."

"So you want me to wait," I guessed.

Austin nodded. "You should wait awhile longer, Leigh," he said.

"but I could end up waiting too long, and then when I go back it might be...too late..."

He and Christina shared a meaningful glance. "Maybe...maybe not," Austin responded.

"Is there something you're not telling me?" I asked suspiciously.

Austin sighed. "Christina and I will tell you everything we know...once we know it."

"And in the meantime?" I prodded.

Austin took a deep breath. "Well, in the meantime, Leigh, you should come and see your— er—mansion."

He and Christina got up, and we walked through the town. After ten minutes I started to see a metallic glimmer in the distance. "What is that?" I questioned.

"Your mansion," was Austin's prompt answer. "It sparkles in the dark."

Presently we came upon the statue of Zach and me, and the three of us paused in silent contemplation.

"I hope he's okay," I said in a soft voice.

"Me too," Christina concurred, her voice wavering. Austin just nodded in agreement, his azure hair gleaming in the starlight (there was no moon out that night, and I wasn't sure if it was a new moon or Vitreusia just didn't have one).

I gazed upon the statue, and remembered Zach's command to me: *"Leigh, go!"* A tear slowly rolled down my cheek. Christina, perceptive as usual, gave me a hug. As I cried, she attempted to comfort me, saying, "It'll be alright, Leigh." I gazed upon the statue of my friend, the tears streaming down my face, and my mind was filled with questions. Was

Zach alright? Had Juliana captured him? Or had his injuries been fatal? What did the look that Austin and Christina exchanged mean?

All these questions resurfaced over and over, and I could not answer them, nor find the answers. The only thing I could do at that point in time…was wait.

Part III:
Writing In The Sky

"This darkness is different. It is powerful, intense—almost impossible to stop."

PROLOGUE.

THEY STARTED OFF NORMAL. About as normal as dreams got, anyways. As I grew older, I noticed that there was one thing each of my dreams had in common: a strange man. His features were always blurred and fuzzy, but somehow I knew that he was young, perhaps in his late twenties or early thirties. He was always involved in my dreams, whether as a mere passerby or an obscure 'relative' that I'd never met.

However, that was not the strange thing about him. The thing that both frightened and intrigued me the most was his voice. It ought to have been strong and vibrant, but was not that in the least.

Instead, his voice sounded old and weak, as if every word he spoke took his last ounce of strength away. A frightening, horrific voice it was, and even in my waking hours the very thought of the sound of it made a shiver run down my spine. And that wasn't all.

The dreams got gradually worse, becoming more frightening every night. I thought about telling someone about them—but they were just nightmares, dreams without any meaning. There was no need to trouble anyone with the strange dreams that filled my head in the night. They went on, progressively getting more upsetting.

One night, I dreamt that I was alone in my room. Suddenly, I heard *his* voice, calling out to me. "Zach…Zach…" Alarmed, I ran out of the room, but the voice followed me, calling, "Zach…Zach…" I sprinted, but that tone still pursued me. At last, I woke up in a cold sweat. It was still dark outside.

When my heart rate had slowed, I went back to sleep and tried not to think about it the following day.

Then, a few nights later, I had my worst nightmare yet. It was almost like a vision, in the sense that I was not physically present. I saw the strange man, lying down in a box made of wood. His eyes were shut.

Suddenly, I felt what he was feeling, saw what he was seeing (I do not know how I knew this). I couldn't breathe, or move. I felt alive, but barely so. I saw…black, with shadows flitting across my line of 'vision', a darker, inky black. And then I heard **his** voice. *"For years I have endured this torture. Help me, Zach, my namesake. Make these accursed shadows leave me!"*

I sat up in my bed, breathing heavily. I knew then that I had to tell someone. And I knew just who to talk to…

I.

Leigh Hollis

I was getting dressed when I heard a knock at the door. "Just a second!" I called as I finished putting on my skirt. I grabbed a brush and began running it through my azure hair. "Come in!" I said. The door opened, and my twin brother Zach ambled into the room.

"Leigh?" he began uncertainly.

"Yes?" I responded nonchalantly.

"Can I talk to you about something?" he asked, running his hand through his wavy azure hair (a nervous tic of his).

I eyed him suspiciously. "Yeeessss?" I said, drawing out the word purposely.

"Um, uh, I've been having really weird dreams." I finished brushing my hair and gave him a sarcastic smirk in response.

"No, Leigh. I'm not kidding around. I'm really not."

Slowly he explained to me the nature of his strange (and creepy) nighttime fantasies.

When he had finished, I looked him in his purple eyes and questioned, "You know who your namesake is, right?"

He nodded. "Zach Dean Johnston. Aunt Leigh's boyfriend."

"Knock it off, you smart aleck!" I retorted. "He was *not* her boyfriend!"

Zach stood up abruptly and went to leave the room. "If you're going to be that way, I guess I'll leave."

"No!" I cried, grabbing him by the shoulder. "We *must* discuss this further!"

"I think I'd rather talk to Mom and Dad about this," he replied.

I snorted. "Oh, really? *That* would be a first."

Zach stopped in the doorway and sighed. "You're right, Leigh," he said. "It would be."

"What do you think the dreams mean?" I inquired.

Zach thought for a moment. "My namesake…he needs my help."

"But *how?*" I queried. "And don't you think we should tell Aunt Leigh about this?"

Zach shook his head. "It could just be my imagination…and in that case, I don't want to give her false hope, although that could be the explanation for the strange actions of his comet…"

"True," I answered. Zach was right.

In Vitreusia, when anyone who has stayed in this

world dies, a comet appears in the sky above where they resided and writes their name in perfect cursive. But that's not all. Every year on the date of their death, the comet reappears and writes their name again. The cycle continues forever. I've seen this spectacle several times, and it is beautiful as well as puzzling.

The odd thing, however, about Zach's comet was that the light faded in, then out again. As a matter of fact, approximately half of his name was visible.

Thinking this over some more, I said, "but how *could* he be—assuming your dreams are correct—half alive?"

"I don't know, Leigh. but I *must* find out what the cause of these dreams is—I don't want to be having nightmares for the rest of my life!"

"Shh!" I warned. "You'll wake them!" (I was referring to our parents)

Zach lowered his voice to a whisper. "We have to do something."

"*We?*" I replied skeptically.

"Yes, *we*," was Zach's rejoinder. "You're the only one I can trust with this. I can't tell anyone—Aunt Leigh would freak out, and our parents would think I was nuts. I have to solve this—whether you will help me or not is up to you."

"I'll help you. You're the only brother I have, and I'm not about to let you embark on a crazy quest all by yourself."

Zach smiled wanly. "I'm glad of that. I'll let you know if I have another—er—stimulating dream."

Then, a voice called from the other end of the
house, making the two of us jump.

"Zach! Leigh! Come on, we're leaving!"

"Ohmygosh!" I exclaimed in realization. Zach
turned around in the doorway.

"What?"

"Today's Mercurii. We're visiting Aunt Leigh!"

"Oh!" he said in surprise. "Darn! We have to get
going, then!" We rushed out of my room and to the
front door.

A suspicious glint was in our mother's purple
eyes, replicas of our own. "What were you two
doing?" she asked.

"Oh...nothing," I spoke up (I was the better liar
of the two of us). "We were just talking."

Our parents shared a knowing smile. Zach and I
had always been close, often taking each other into
confidence before our parents.

"Well!" our dad said suddenly. "We had better be
going—Leigh will think something has happened to
us on the way." Zach's eyes opened wide. "Yikes. We
should hurry."

We speed walked the whole way, passing by the
marble tribute to Zach and I's namesakes. After a
brisk five minutes' walk, we arrived at Aunt Leigh's
manor, which glimmered metallic silver in the
sunlight. Mom took a deep breath and knocked on
the door.

In less than a minute it was opened by Aunt
Leigh (she lived alone). Aunt Leigh actually wasn't
Zach and I's actual 'aunt', but she and our parents

were so close that we had grown up calling her that. She was super pretty, with deep, gorgeous blue eyes and a shimmering mane of long black hair.

On the other hand, a constant grief shone through her eyes. Our parents told Zach and I that Aunt Leigh missed Zach—my brother's namesake—an awful lot, and that was why she always looked a little bit sad.

For as long as I could remember, Zach and I had been admonished by our parents to be careful of what we said around Aunt Leigh, and not to ask too many questions, for fear of upsetting her. Honestly, I liked her, I really did, but I'd never shaken that feeling of cautiousness around her, and Zach felt the same way.

As she led us into the large kitchen, I carefully sealed my lips and made sure there was no chance of Zach's secret slipping out of them. "How are my twins?" Aunt Leigh asked as she stirred a saucepan full of calii (a warm, spicy drink—a Vitreusian recipe thousands of years old).

"We're good," Zach and I answered simultaneously (this happens quite often, actually, and we almost never do it on purpose—really!).

Aunt Leigh smiled and poured the calii into five mugs. "I was hoping you four could help me with some renovations."

"Like what, Leigh?" inquired Mom.

Aunt Leigh tapped her fingers on her chin. "Well, I was thinking Austin and Zach could help rearrange the furniture and trim the shrubbery…and then the kitchen needs to be reorganized."

Mom nodded. "Sure, we can do that for you."

Aunt Leigh shook her head vigorously as she finished off her calii. "No, no! I' m not going to sit around while the four of you do all the work! The only reason I ask you to help is because I…can't…do it…by myself…"

As she said the last six words, her speech slowed down, and her voice became choked.

Both of my parents looked on her with sympathetic eyes. "We understand completely, Leigh," Mom said softly as she got up and began to clear the table.

Our visit lasted a good four hours, most of which I spent cleaning and organizing cupboards. My dad and Zach did a lot of heavy lifting, and when we got back home, Zach was exhausted (he had gotten up early due to his dream).

While he napped, I sat in my room and practiced my calligraphy (my least favorite subject at school— thankfully, I only had a few months of it to go). I wrote the letters slowly and painstakingly (which with my attention span and energy level, is pretty darn near impossible).

I was in the middle of writing a fancy *f* when Zach burst into the room.

I jumped straight up, and my pen made a straight line down my paper. "Leigh," he whispered, his voice low and upset, his purple eyes panicky and as big as marbles.

"What is it?" I queried, rolling up my paper and putting away both it and the pen.

He swallowed hard, looking me in my purple eyes, exact copies of his own. "I had another dream," he said.

II.

Zach Easton

"I was walking towards the Cliffs of Fate, and I went through an orchard and a gorge…then I climbed up the cliffs and there were letters carved into rock. They said, **Darren Von Fare.** There were several caves there, one of which I entered. I came upon a steel door, which was wide open. It led into a medium sized room, which was empty except for some broken chains lying on the floor. I walked straight towards the other side of the room, and there was a square carved into the wall with circular impressions that looked like buttons, and inside of those were carved roman numerals. I pressed, in order, three, one, and six, and a section of the wall creaked and swung forward. Cautiously making my way into the secret room, I discovered a book, which looked very old. It glowed faintly and had a strange musty, sharp sort of smell. I reached for it, about to pick it up, but then I heard Zach's—at least I *hope* it's Zach's—voice and I stopped. He said: 'Follow the directions which I have given you, and you will find the book which will tell you how to revive me.'"

Leigh stood up abruptly and began throwing some things into a burlap sack—her bow, a bunch of arrows, some water, a wooden whistle. Throwing the pack over her shoulder, she ordered: "Get your bow and arrow—quickly. I will wait for you here."

"Wait a minute!" I protested. "Exactly what do you think we are going to do here?"

Leigh's expression was firm, her purple eyes determined. "We're going to find that book, of course." I groaned inwardly. Leigh had set her mind on going to find the book, and when my sister makes up her mind to do something, she is more stubborn than…well, a mule.

"Come on, Leigh, you can't be serious about this. It's dangerous and if something happens to us no one will know where we've gone."

Leigh whirled around, her blue hair flying. She gave me a challenging look as she came back with, "I thought you didn't like nightmares."

"I don't!" I insisted.

"Well then!" My stubborn, headstrong twin sister huffed. "We had better get going!"

Throwing my hands up in exasperation, I went to my room and grabbed my bow and some arrows. We rushed, hastily yet quietly, out the door and headed for the Cliffs of Fate. As we walked towards them, Leigh started to grow uncomfortable.

"Zach?" she asked.

"What?" I answered.

"You—you know what happened around here, right?"

I took a deep breath and let it out. "It was something with my namesake."

Leigh's purple eyes flashed, and she was about to interrupt me, but I beat her to talking. "Whoa, sis. Hang on a second there. I know…what happened here, but that doesn't mean I like talking about it."

Leigh's eyes narrowed. "Just tell me, so I know you're right."

"My namesake and yours were in the gorge up ahead when they ran into Darren…and Zach was shot."

"That's right," Leigh affirmed slowly. For the next minute or two we were silent, and Leigh broke that silence by saying, "You're freaked out, aren't you?"

I swallowed hard. "How did you know?"

Her purple eyes bored into me. "Because. I just do."

"Well if we're playing 'guess how your twin is feeling' then you're freaked out, too."

Leigh played with her azure hair nervously. "I am, Zach."

"I think I know why, too, because it's the exact same reason I'm uncomfortable."

"That the last time two people named Zach and Leigh walked through *this* gorge, one of them died?"

"That'd be it."

We fell into an unpleasant stillness again, and this time it lasted until we were right up by the cliffs—the Cliffs of Fate. "We climb up these over here, right?" Leigh asked, pointing to a spot where the cliffs weren't so steep and looked somewhat scalable.

I looked at them for a moment or two, matching them to the cliffs in my dream. "Uhh..yeah." and up we went.

It was a grueling task climbing up them, and both Leigh and I nearly slipped to our deaths several times, but in the end we made it.

We pulled ourselves up over the precipice, gasping and panting. Leigh's arms were scratched, and I could see a bruise forming on her forehead. I gave myself a once-over and saw that I was cut and bruised as well. "Where to next?" Leigh panted, adjusting her knapsack.

I looked around, and my eyes alighted upon three words carved into the rock—the same ones I had seen in my dream. **Darren Von Fare.** I walked over to them and surveyed the caves. They looked like old, abandoned mines. I closed my eyes and replayed the scene in my dream in which I had entered one of the caves. Opening them again, I pointed to one of the dark, rectangular entrances.

"This one. I went through this one."

A glint of fear appeared in Leigh's eyes, there one moment, gone the next. "Let's go," she said decisively, heading for the opening, and I took a few long strides to keep up with her. The cave was dark, and we wandered down a corridor that twisted and turned, with no light to see by but our faintly glowing selves.

We encountered a metal door—the exact one I had seen in my dream. It was open, and, taking deep breaths, Leigh and I walked through it. I strode over to the opposite wall, and there was the square carving with the buttons. I looked at it thoroughly, verifying that this was, indeed, the same thing I had seen in my dream. Then I pressed the buttons. *Three, one, six.*

A door became visible and swung out towards Leigh and I with an immense *creak!*

However, just as I was considering jumping out of the way, it came to an abrupt stop. Together we entered the secret room. It was long and narrow, and in the right-hand corner an old book glowed faintly. I smelled the same musty, sharp smell that I had smelled in my dream.

"This is it," I whispered to Leigh as we approached it cautiously.

Carefully, I picked the book up and opened it. It was written in the fanciest cursive you could ever imagine, and I recognized it at once. *Calligraphy.* Unfortunately, I couldn't read it, because calligraphy was my worst subject, and I could barely write it well enough to get by.

"What does it say?" I inquired of Leigh in a low tone (she wasn't great at calligraphy, either, but she was a good deal better than I was.).

"It says…the manuscript of Vitreusia—The Book of Laws."

"Huh," was my intelligent response. "Is there a

table of contents or an index?"

Leigh carefully flipped through the first few pages. "Nope."

I groaned. "We'll have to look through it page by page."

Slowly, Leigh turned the pages, reading me short blurbs from them. The book was both strange and interesting at the same time—the illustrations in it seemed to animate themselves. There was a whole section on Vitreusian history, and Leigh made short work of that. Like our father, she had both a love for Vitreusian history and a knack for memorizing it all.

The next section appeared to be about the void—which neither Leigh nor I had ever been in. She swiftly turned the pages, pausing for a moment on a page that looked particularly interesting. The illustrations depicted two people, one on either page. One of them had a tree-like look to him, with brownish-gray skin and hair and eyes the color of spring leaves. He stared off into the distance, a peculiar twinkle in his eyes.

The other being, a girl, had an altogether different manifestation. Her skin was a rich olive tone, her eyes an inky black. Her sleek, straight, shining black hair just brushed her shoulder, and two flawless braids were on either side of the sides of her head. An odd aura emitted from her—instead of the distinctive Vitreusian glow, it was as if a jet-black mist emitted from her body. She stared off the page and seemingly right at me.

Then, her image began to animate. Her eyes

turned from black to blue, blue to yellow, yellow to orange, and orange to red. Then she winked at me, her eyes returning to their original color. I turned to Leigh, who was also looking intently at the images on the two pages. "What are these pictures of?" I asked.

Leigh scanned the pages for an instant. "The girl is a resident of the Republic of Noxa. The boy is from the Sylvanian Democracy."

"Um…okay," I responded confusedly as she turned the page.

"If you paid attention in history class you'd know what I was talking about," Leigh said pointedly, beginning to flip quickly through the book once more.

I sighed and resolved to try my best *not* to fall asleep in history class next time. "Is there any sign of what we're looking for yet? Anything on the water of life or a recipe for a resurrection potion, perhaps?"

"Not yet—" Leigh started to answer, and then a loud ***boom!*** cut her off. "What was that?" Leigh said, her voice trembling.

"Could it have been—"

I began, and apparently we were thinking the same thing because Leigh interrupted me, saying, "Oh, **no,**" and together we ran for the door we had come through.

Sure enough, the stone slab of a door had fallen off its rusted hinges and now completely blocked the entryway. *"This can't be!"* I thought to myself. but it was. I could feel my sister's heart beating rapidly in the narrow space. I gulped and faced her just as she faced me.

"We're—we're.." I stammered, completely at a loss for words.

"Trapped," Leigh declared, completing my unfinished sentence.

III.

Leigh Kline

I was just sitting down to supper when there was a loud knock at the door. I got up immediately and opened it.

Christina and Austin were on the other side, and they both looked panicked. "Leigh," Christina said, struggling for breath, "have you seen the twins?"

"No…" I answered slowly. "Why do you ask?"

"We've been looking for them everywhere, but we can't find them," Austin stated seriously.

"We're worried that they're hurt or lost!" Christina put in, her voice shaking.

I gripped the door jamb for support. "Please, not the twins, too!" I whispered to no one in particular. Then I looked Christina in the eye. "I'll help you look for them," I told her. "Just let me grab my dagger."

I was back with it in less than a minute, and I came out of the house, closing the door behind me.

"Where should we search for them first?" I inquired of Austin and Christina.

Austin thought for a moment. "We've already scoured the house and the town…so I say we go to Glass Mountain first and the Cliffs of Fate second."

I took a deep breath. "Alright, let's go."

We headed to Glass Mountain. The day was bright, and the light reflecting off the nearly transparent mountain made all of us squint as we headed towards it.

A memory came back to me, a breath of nostalgia drifting past.

Zach took my hand and kissed it with the utmost respect and reverence. "I will defend you to the end, Leigh."

Christina spoke up. "So will I."

"I will too," said Austin solemnly, and in one swift motion they were all on one knee before me.

Pushing the memory to the back of my mind, I began ascending the mountain, Christina to my left, Austin to my right. It was slow going, but at last we made it to the cave—the very same cave in which Darren had wounded and abducted Austin and Christina. My heart rate rose as we entered the dark cave—I couldn't help it.

When I glanced at Christina and Austin they appeared nervous as well, and I certainly didn't blame them. Every step brought Christina's frantic scream back into my ears. Soon, though, we saw a light at the end of the passage, and all of us began to relax slightly. In less than five minutes Austin, Christina and I stood at the edge of a cliff.

After taking in the view, we started to make our way down from where the cliff wasn't as steep. By this time, both Christina and Austin had an alarmed look to them, and they held each other's hands tightly.

We silently headed towards the Cliffs of Fate, and I began to be assaulted by my memory. As much as I tried to keep the flashbacks from appearing in my mind's eye, I couldn't stop them.

When we began walking through the gorge, I started to feel dizzy and lightheaded. I could feel myself swaying like a palm tree in a hurricane, but I couldn't balance myself. When I looked up, I could almost swear that I saw Darren's tall, slender silhouette. My mind tricked me into thinking that I had just heard his terrifying laugh...my footsteps slowed. I knew I was approaching the spot where Zach had been shot.

My vision grew blurry, and everything began to fade away into black. Then a number of images flashed before my eyes: Zach giving me the necklace and dagger. *"Rise, Leigh Kaitlyn Kline, 23rd in the line of Vitreusia's heroes!"* Zach and I talking on top of Glass Mountain. *"It's probably just me, but I've always had that feeling, like I'm ridiculously out of my league."* Zach leaping in front of me, taking the arrow for me, and falling to the ground...*"I will defend you to the end, Leigh."* Lastly, his last words to me before he was rushed away by doctors and nurses. *"Be strong, Leigh. Be strong for me."* Then I saw his name, half-written across the sky like it was annually. And I heard his voice. *"Leigh...look for the children where you found their parents."*

The image died away, and I opened my eyes to see Christina and Austin standing over me. Both of their visages were awash with concern. Christina spoke first.

"Leigh, are you alright?" Slowly, I sat up. My head ached slightly.

"Yeah…I'm okay," I answered. "I think I know where to look for the twins."

"You do?" Austin and Christina inquired together.

"Yes. Follow me."

I initiated the taxing climb up the Cliffs of Fate, and Austin and Christina followed. It was not until we hoisted ourselves onto the top, panting and sweaty, that either of them questioned my unexpected information. "How do you know where to look for the twins?" Christina queried, gasping for air.

Quickly I relayed the details of my flashbacks, and what I hoped was a revelation from Zach and not a figment of my imagination. What I didn't tell them, though, is that I'd had similar experiences to this beforehand. Whenever I was at my lowest point and feeling lonely, sad, and despondent, an encouraging message would write itself across the sky. They were short but sweet, and they always used my name, so I knew they were for me—but as to who was conveying these messages to me, not a single clue was to be found.

For example, one night the tears would not stop flowing down my face. It was as if a switch had been turned on and I couldn't turn it off. Over and over Zach's last command played in my head: *"Leigh, go!"* I stepped out onto the balcony, trying to escape the pain that was taking me over from the inside out. And then these words were written in stardust across the sky: "Don't cry, Leigh." Swiftly, I felt better, less sad.

That was only one of the times I received encouragement from the heavens. I'm not saying or even implying that it wasn't hard (living in Vitreusia without Zach). but those mysterious correspondences…well, they helped a lot. I *would* tell Austin and Christina about them, eventually—but now was not the time. Promptly, silently, I headed for the mines.

A shudder ran down my spine as I looked at the jagged words, carved into the rock years ago: **Darren Von Fare.** "This way," I said to Austin and Christina, walking into one of the yawning doorways.

They glanced at each other uncertainly, then followed me. After striding down the narrow passage, we came to a metal door—the same metal door which I had opened with my dagger to rescue Christina and Austin years ago. The three of us proceeded cautiously into the room, which, at first glance, appeared to be empty. "Leigh!" Austin shouted earnestly.

"Zach!" Christina called not five seconds afterwards. A muffled yell came from the wall opposite us.

"Mom! Dad! Over here!" *The twins!* We sprinted over to where the noise had come from.

A large stone slab leaned against a rectangular opening, sealing all but a small sliver of it off from us. "We're stuck behind this door," said Leigh, her voice shaking.

"Don't worry, dears," Christina reassured both of her children. "We'll have you out in no time." Together the three of us shifted the slab, creating an aperture just large enough to allow the twins to emerge from their stony prison. Leigh carried a large, faintly glowing book, which she set down upon squeezing through the gap to embrace me and her parents.

A feeling of relief engulfed the room, and Austin spoke up. "What in the name of all twenty-three liberators are you two *doing* here??" Zach bit his lip nervously, but a bold gleam shone through Leigh's grape-juice purple eyes, exact replicas of Christina's. "Zach," she urged, "You have to tell them."

Austin raised an eyebrow. "What—" he began, but Leigh interrupted him.

"Zach has to tell you something—all of you." Austin, Christina and I shared a glance. Christina's face betrayed worry, and Austin's expression denoted both confusion and concern.

Zach took a deep breath and started to talk—and as he got further on through his narrative, my heart began to beat faster. When I stole a few glances at Christina and Austin, their faces indicated both shock and hope—the exact same emotions that pulsed through my head when Zach finished his astonishing tale. Zach looked to me as if to say, 'please weigh in on this situation.' "Well," I said uncertainly, my voice wavering, "Have you found the information in this book that pertains to—to what's going on here?"

Leigh shook her head. "No, not yet. We were about two-thirds of the way through the book when—when the door fell off its hinges."

"Let's look through it some more, then," Austin said resolutely.

Zach set the book down on the stony floor, and we began to leaf through it.

"This book dates back to the antediluvian days of Vitreusia—many, many millenniums ago." Austin whispered in awe. "Incredible. To think I was once steps away from such an amazing historical artifact!" Leigh flipped the pages, scanning each one quickly.

"No…no…no…aha!" she exclaimed at last, stopping on an abundantly illustrated page.

"What? What does it say?" I asked eagerly (Vitreusian calligraphy was my nemesis—just looking at the stuff made my head hurt).

"It says…" Leigh said slowly, studying the elaborate script, "a complete guide to the revival of one who has forfeited their own life for another."

I swallowed hard. Zach fit that description perfectly. Then Leigh gasped—a gasp that conveyed astonishment and disappointment at the same time.

"What is it, Leigh?" inquired Christina fearfully.

"It—it says here," Leigh stammered, looming tears choking her voice, "that the procedure is only possible with someone hailing from Vitreusia, the Sylvanian Democracy, or the Republic of Noxa.

Earthly beings…cannot be resurrected—no matter whether they sacrificed their lives or not."

Just like that, all my hopes were crushed, and I let out a sigh of despair. But that feeling was short lived, for I quickly realized that the situation simply did not make sense. "Wait a minute," I said slowly, thinking each word through.

"This isn't right. If Zach was *truly* mortal, he wouldn't be able to show up in Zach's dreams. It wouldn't be doable for him to—to manipulate comets! There *has* to be something we're missing!"

Christina, Austin, Zach, and Leigh all looked at me, their expressions both surprised and wary.

"What did you say, Leigh?" Austin asked. "Something about controlling comets?" I rocked back and forth on my knees, so absorbed in thought that I hardly heard him. I racked my brain for any possible clue…and suddenly I had it.

I opened my eyes and glanced at Leigh, then Austin. "I think I have the missing piece to this puzzle."

IV.

Leigh Hollis

Slowly, the story of the mysterious circumstances which led to Zach's (Aunt Leigh's friend, not my brother) adoption poured out of Aunt Leigh's lips. She was close to finishing up her tale when the explanation occurred to me. I smiled in spite of myself and glanced over at my dad to see if he had figured it out as well.

Sure enough, he mouthed to me: "I've got it." and then turned his focus to Aunt Leigh once more.

"And that's all I know," Aunt Leigh finished.

My dad spoke first. "Leigh, my daughter and I know what happened concerning Zach."

Aunt Leigh's features were a mixture of concern and excitement as she appealed, "Please tell me." Dad motioned at me with his hand as if to say "you're on."

I cleared my throat. "Aunt Leigh, it appears that my brother's namesake is an inter duos."

194

Aunt Leigh looked confused. "I've done my best to educate myself regarding the Vitreusian language and terms, but this expression is not familiar to me. Please explain yourself."

I was silent for a moment or two, putting the clarification together in my head. "The exact translation of inter duos is 'between the two'. Inter duos is used to describe someone whose parents were both mortal and Vitreusian. In Zach's case, his mother was born on Earth, but his father was from Vitreusia. Someone who is an inter duos...well, I'll just say it's not an easy life.

There haven't been many cases of inter duos—perhaps a hundred in Vitreusia's history, and maybe there were a few other occurrences that weren't recorded. You see, the very blood of an inter duos is at war with itself—a constant conflict between genetics never truly meant to be mixed together. I'd compare it to the practice called genetic engineering in your home world, where, say, the genetics of fish are added to corn. Inter duos are a lot like that. There are certainly advantages to being half Vitreusian, half mortal—but there are certain drawbacks as well."

I could see Aunt Leigh processing it all, the thoughtful look in her blue eyes as she said, "Go on."

So I continued: "One of the disadvantages is, as I said before, that from the very beginning, there is a conflict within the very fiber of your being—bone against bone, blood against blood. This makes inter duos feel as if they don't actually belong anywhere, because when the Vitreusian genetics are at peace in

Vitreusia, the mortal part feels considerable unrest.

Now, regular mortals can be contented in Vitreusia—because there isn't a continual battle raging inside of them which pits one world in opposition to another. Also, this internal collision makes an inter duos extremely vulnerable to any type of illness, and if the immune system is not strengthened regularly, the consequences could be fatal."

"Thank you, Leigh," my dad said when I took a breath of air. "I'll take it from here. What this means is that the revival process will, in fact, work. It also explains the strange circumstances of Zach's present consciousness. I cannot explain that, for to my knowledge, it has never transpired before in the history of Vitreusia.

The important thing, though, is that the procedure will work—provided that this book is a reliable source—and my knowledge of such matters tells me it is."

Aunt Leigh's blue eyes sparkled with hope. "Let's see what the book says, then!"

"By all means," Dad replied, putting the glowing tome in the center of our five-person circle. Everyone looked at me expectantly.

"Am I supposed to be the one reading?" I asked, somewhat perplexed. Surely Mom or Dad could read calligraphy more effectively than I could, but apparently they couldn't, for they gave me the go-ahead. "Uhh…okay," I said softly, trying to find where I was in the book.

It took me awhile, but after a minute or two I began to read: "Go through the Valley of Cheer, over Courage Mountain, and through the forest of Ethereality to find the Tree of Vitality. To get the sap which will restore your friend, you must induce its keeper, not by violence or threats, but by benevolence and shrewdness of tongue, to give you some sap from the Tree of Revival.

When you have obtained for yourself a vial of the precious sap, let a drop fall onto the center of the blank area below, and you will receive further instructions. And of course, that's where it ends, and the rest of the page is blank."

My brother's lips were set in a thin, grim line. "So…where are the 'Valley of Cheer' and 'Courage Mountain' and the 'forest of Ethereality'?" My parents exchanged a glance, and I at once knew they recognized these places and were aware of their locations…but for some reason, they were reluctant to reveal this information.

"Mom, Dad," I said cautiously, "What are you not telling us?"

My dad threw my mom another momentary look as he turned to Aunt Leigh, my brother and I and said, "All three of these landforms are in the Sylvanian Democracy."

I swallowed, for I immediately recognized the name. "The what?"

"The Sylvanian Democracy. Another world, almost opposite ours. It can be accessed from the void, but both it and its inhabitants are rather…different from Vitreusia."

I turned to Zach. "The picture," we said at the same time.

My dad's eyebrow went up. "What—?"

"Never mind," I said quickly, the words stumbling off my tongue.

He continued, "Although the people of the Sylvanian Democracy and Vitreusia have always gotten along rather well, our paths have not crossed for hundreds of years. Hazarding a trip there is risky and possibly deadly, as we have no idea what could lie on the other side. They may have forgotten that we exist, and a visit from us—or anyone, for that matter, might not be welcome." He paused for a couple moments, then continued, "Also, there is a—very slight—possibility that the Noxans have wiped them out."

Zach's eyes grew large. "The—the Noxans?" he stuttered.

"Yes," Dad answered. "The Noxans—a hostile, arrogant, sturdy race. The people of darkness and the night. Since the beginning of time, they have been unpleasant towards both our people and those of the Sylvanian Democracy. Millennia ago, we sealed Vitreusia from them—if the Sylvanians were unable to do the same, their world may be nothing but a sea of darkness and confusion now."

Zach shook his head. "I don't believe it," he muttered quietly.

Dad stood up, a serious expression on his face. "That being said, I refuse to go through with this

procedure—or to even permit any of you to imperil yourselves in a trip to the Sylvanian Democracy."
I could see my mom out of the corner of my eye, and I could tell just by looking at her that she agreed with Dad. Aunt Leigh's blue eyes had tears in them, and she had a defeated air.

However, that soon changed. Her dark eyebrows knit together, and she rose up abruptly. "Zach risked—and eventually gave up—his life for me. If I were not willing to do the same for him, would I be honoring his sacrifice—or the legacy that he left behind?" She pronounced each word clearly, without a single pause or waver in tone. I had never seen her so resolute.

My parents were shocked. They held each other's gaze for a while, as if asking each other for advice. And in that moment, I made up my mind as well and got up off the floor. "I will accompany my namesake." Mom's jaw was about to drop, but she caught herself just in time.
Zach fixated his purple eyes upon me, asking a silent question. *"Should I go with you two?"*
I flashed him a response. *"Absolutely."* So my brother arose as well.
"I will go with them." he said firmly. And for the first time in a long, long, long time, both of my parents were at a loss for words.

V.

Zach Easton

Okay, so I normally don't make firm stands like that, especially when neither of my parents are on my side, but the thought of having those awful nightmares for the rest of my life was pretty scary. Much scarier than being grounded for a few weeks or whatever punishment my parents would come up with (assuming we all got back alive).

Besides the nightmare factor, I really wanted to help Aunt Leigh revive Zach regardless. And on a selfish note, I had always been jealous of Leigh, because her namesake was alive and well. To be able to finally talk to and interact with my namesake...the experience would be priceless. I glanced at my parents, who had locked eyes. I could tell they were stuck between a rock and a hard place. Finally my dad broke the uncomfortable silence. "Christina and I will let you go."

"Oh, thank you," Aunt Leigh gushed, her eyes shining.

"We must keep this excursion a secret from everyone besides ourselves," my mom put in. "Eventually, we will tell all of them the truth. For now, though, we will hide some things in the closet, so to speak."

Aunt Leigh nodded. "Let's prepare for our trip, then."

"There's not much else for us to bring," my sister said. "Zach and I have our bows and arrows, and we already have the book. All we need is some extra arrows and some provisions."

Dad's face was grim. "I would not bring weapons into the Sylvanian Democracy."

Leigh looked confused, and I was sure my countenance bore a similar expression. "The Sylvanians were—and likely still are—a peace-loving people. It took years for us Vitreusians to convince them to take up arms against the Noxans to prevent both our worlds from being wiped out by their dark forces. The president of their nation always had bodyguards, but as a population, ninety percent of them didn't own any weapons whatsoever.

It wasn't that it was hard or illegal to get or possess a weapon—it wasn't that at all. The people simply didn't want them nor did they feel like they had any need for them. Believe it or not, there's hardly any crime committed there. However, if you three show up with daggers and bows and arrows, they will likely be frightened and resort to violent conduct."

Leigh pursed her lips. "I still think we should take our weapons.What if the Noxans have taken over? We'll have to fight them."

"If the Noxans have taken over," my dad said firmly, "the land will be a shapeless mass of darkness and disorder. Any preexisting landforms will have vanished completely. You will not fight them, for alone you will surely be defeated. You will leave that land at once. Later on, we could attempt to rip Sylvania from the Noxans' grasp…but later on. You do not need your weapons. Leigh can bring her dagger—but that's all. Understood?" The three of us nodded.

◆ ◆ ◆

Packing for our precarious excursion took five minutes, maybe less. After all, the only things we were bringing were some provisions and Aunt Leigh's dagger—the latter she already had with her. We briefly consulted the book for the chant to get into the Sylvanian Democracy, and then we headed for the void. Leigh and I's parents spoke in low tones to Aunt Leigh, and then turned to my sister, talking to her briefly. Then they came over to me.

"Be careful, Zach," Mom pleaded worriedly, giving me a quick peck on the cheek.

I bit my lip. "I will."

Dad gave me a brief hug. "Watch where you tread, buddy," he said with a faint smile that only partly covered up his concern.

"I will, Dad," I answered seriously. Then he and Mom left, and it was just Aunt Leigh, Leigh and me. We exchanged looks and began walking through the void.

We had walked for just a few minutes when Aunt Leigh stopped abruptly and chanted: "In pace no in bello, venia…O terram aperi." A rectangle of blackness shimmered and faded away, revealing a wooded land. The sky was pitch-black, without any stars to be seen.

We stepped in, and the void slowly vanished into thin air. It was extremely dark, and my eyes took awhile to adjust to the dimness.

When they did, I caught my breath. A tall, slender, humanlike figure was making its way through the woods. I gulped and tapped Aunt Leigh on the shoulder. I motioned to her to be quiet and pointed at the mysterious profile. Whatever or whoever it was turned, and I saw the outline of a bow. Quickly I glanced at my sister. Her wide purple eyes told me all I needed to know. She had seen it too. Then I noticed something very disturbing.

The figure emanated darkness. It swirled around the person's form, making the dark forest even darker. It was as if that individual was the embodiment of darkness itself. Suddenly my father's voice rang in my mind's ears. *The Noxans—a hostile, arrogant, sturdy race. The people of darkness and the night."* The mysterious person was a Noxan!

No sooner had I come to this realization than the figure whirled, apparently somehow sensing our presence, and made a throwing motion towards the three of us. Suddenly my eyes failed me, and my senses faded. I felt like a cold clammy blanket was being wrapped tightly around me. I realized that I was being enveloped in darkness...and that was my last thought before consciousness left me.

When I came to, the first face I saw was of a grayish shade, with a shock of green hair and vibrant green eyes. *"A Sylvanian,"* I thought groggily. *"The Noxans haven't taken over after all."* My relief was short-lived, however, for the stranger began to speak, and in an unfriendly tone. "I am President Tahigwa Salomos of the Sylvanian Democracy, and I demand to know what you intruders are doing in my nation."

VI.

Leigh Kline

I got to my feet, my head still spinning from our encounter with the Noxan. "We come in peace," I managed to say.

President Tahigwa's green eyes narrowed. "So you say. but peaceful visitors make themselves known at once, rather than sneaking around. My attendants and I heard rustling in the brush, but were not concerned by it, thinking it was one of the many creatures to be found in our woods. Now I realize, though, that the three of you were the ones making the noise."

I swallowed hard. "President Tahigwa, please let me speak. We are on an important mission to save a friend of mine, and we had to come here—there was no other way. We had no idea as to whether your land was still intact and what traditions are followed here. Please forgive us, it was an honest mistake."

He scoffed. "Honest! Everyone who comes through this land says they are honest! The Noxans assured my ancestors of their integrity, and later waged war upon our land!"

I thought of the Noxan who had cloaked us in darkness—he or she was probably roaming through the woods at this very moment.

"President Tahigwa!" Leigh spoke up. "Please listen to me. The Noxans have returned to your land! We met one just a few feet from where you're standing! He or she knocked us out and vanished! I hope you believe us, President—we're the good guys."

He studied her closely. "Are you…a Vitreusian?"

Leigh nodded. "Yes. And this is my brother, who is also a Vitreusian," she said, gesturing to Zach.

President Tahigwa set his eyes upon me, a suspicious look on his face. "You're not a Vitreusian, and I can see you're not a Noxan. Who are you, then?"

Since I could tell frankness was a must here, I told him the truth (and I also saw no reason to lie to him, either). "I am from Earth, or, as the Vitreusians say, Terra."

President Tahigwa's face was grim. "Terrans are a greedy, selfish, and arrogant people. They are not to be trusted," he muttered, more to himself than to me. "Guards!" he cried, and his muscular companions snapped to attention. "Take these three to court at once! I must gather my officials!" He glared at us. "We will show them how Sylvanians deal with trespassers."

◆◆◆

Just a few hours ago I had been going about my life in Vitreusia as usual…but now I stood with my friends' twins, Zach and Leigh, in a foreign (and openly hostile) court.

There were over one hundred people in the ancient structure, all of whom looked rather treelike, with skin that resembled bark and eyes and hair the color of summer leaves. They murmured among themselves, eyeing us resentfully. "I'm not entirely sure," Leigh whispered in my ear in a softly sarcastic tone, "but I think they don't like us."

I glanced around the imposing room and its infuriated inhabitants and grimaced. "Don't like is probably an understatement," I whispered back.

A loud *dong* coming from the bell in the center of the ceiling silenced everyone. The President appeared, apparently emerging from a secret passage of sorts. He had changed into a long red robe, and a gold circlet now rested upon his head. "My good people," he said solemnly. "While performing the monthly twilight ritual I came upon three prowlers, taking refuge in our very own woods!" Unhappy chatter filled the room, bouncing off the walls that were yellowed with age.

President Tahigwa raised his hand in a mute plea for silence. "Please, calm yourselves. Justice will be served. I present to you the interlopers!" he announced, motioning to Zach, Leigh and I.

The room erupted with anger. Shouted curses filled the air. Everywhere I looked, fists were shaking and eyes were flashing heatedly.

President Tahigwa glanced around the room, a satisfied look on his face. Then he stretched his arms out and shouted over the chaos, "Enough! I will have stillness in the court!" And at once, it was quiet. "I will tell you my story. I came upon these three asleep in the woods-our woods!" shouts of protest rang out, and President Tahigwa held up his hand for peace. "Upon their awakening, they insisted that they came in peace and meant no harm. But who has ever met an honest trespasser?"

The people responded together: "Not I!"

President Tahigwa nodded his affirmation and continued, "Indeed, I know what they are up to. The oldest among them is from that dreadful and wicked realm of Terra. She has sweet-talked these young Vitreusians into collaborating with her to take over the Sylvanian Democracy!"

Once again, the people began to yell and shout. I stole a glance at the twins. Zach looked pale and frightened.

Leigh, however, just looked mad—just as incensed as the Sylvanians, if not even more so. She flipped her blue tresses indignantly, and her purple eyes flashed as she cried, "People of the Sylvanian Democracy!" At once everyone was silent, and over a hundred pairs of green eyes focused upon Leigh. "My namesake has already said this to your president, and I will say it again! We come in peace!"

"Yeah, right!" a tall, plump fellow snarled.

"How do we know you're telling the truth?" challenged a woman with white birch-like skin. The whole crowd yelled in agreement.

"Enough!" President Tahigwa hollered. "Who pronounces them…" here he looked about the room with a triumphant air, "guilty as charged."

There ensued such a racket the likes of which I had never heard before in my life. Zach was as white as a sheet.

"I think it's unanimous," he murmured to Leigh and I.

I was about to respond when President Tahigwa started to speak once more. "I suggest deporting the Vitreusians…" here cheers erupted from the crowd, and the president smiled. "…and as for the perpetrator of this situation, she shall be.." here he paused dramatically, "executed." The building shook with the applause and shouted approval. Zach's knees began to shake, and Leigh steadied him. "Guards!" President Tahigwa called. "Bind the criminals. Then we will carry out the sentences."

They advanced towards us, and although I knew what I was about to do would not help our cause, I did it anyway. Zach had to be saved…and with that thought, I drew my dagger from its sheath.

VII.

Leigh Hollis

Aunt Leigh crouched, the jewels on her dagger gleaming. The guards moved towards us, ready for a fight—a fight, I was sure, that they would win. but just as Aunt Leigh lowered her dagger, preparing for one last stand, President Tahigwa cried out, "Stop! Nobody move!" The guards froze, and so did Aunt Leigh.

President Tahigwa quickly descended from his podium and dashed over to Aunt Leigh, his green eyebrows knit. He made a motion to the guards to back off and went down on one knee before Aunt Leigh. "I have made a grave mistake," he said, bowing his head. "I beg your forgiveness, salvator." Zach and I made eye contact, and I'm sure I looked just as confused to him as he did to me.

"Ignosco tibi," Aunt Leigh responded. *I forgive you.*

Then she said, "Surgere quaeso." *Please rise.*

President Tahigwa did, and turned to the crowd, which had begun whispering among themselves. "My people! I have made a great mistake! Standing before us is the liberator of Vitreusia itself! They are not criminals, but rather our honored guests. Please treat them as such."

The Sylvanian's facial expressions changed from "I wish you were dead" to "Maybe you're not my worst enemy". "Court dismissed," President Tahigwa said, clapping his hands. Then he turned to the three of us. "Please, come with me."

We followed him to an impressive mansion, whose exterior was decorated with painted trees.

He walked up to the door and stretched out his hand. Twigs emerged from it, twisting into an intricate key, which he used to unlock the door. He motioned for us to go in ahead of him, and we did, Aunt Leigh leading the way. "Please, sit down," he urged. So we seated ourselves. "First," President Tahigwa began, "please just call me by my first name..adding President complicates things, and besides, I'm only the Sylvanian Democracy's President."

"Tahigwa," Aunt Leigh began, "we are looking for the Valley of Cheer, Courage Mountain, and the forest of Ethereality."

Tahigwa (man, what a bizarre name) scratched his head and answered, "I know where they are. Perhaps I should go with you."

"Oh, no," Aunt Leigh replied. "That won't be

necessary—after all, you have a country to look after. I'm sure if you just provide us with a map we'll be fine."

but Tahigwa shook his head. "Those landforms are very difficult to navigate, even for someone like me who's lived here his whole life. You could get lost or even killed. And besides, I owe you all one for being so unwelcoming and cynical." Here he looked down, obviously ashamed of himself. It was then that I realized he seemed to be no older than twenty-two, and was actually quite handsome when he wasn't sentencing someone to death.

That thought came and went, and Tahigwa started to speak again. "I feel I should explain my wary attitude."

"If it makes you feel better," Aunt Leigh responded kindly (dang, she was a true diplomat).

Tahigwa nodded and took a deep breath, making eye contact with each of us and then looking away again. "The Sylvanian Democracy and the Republic of Noxa have been at war for many, many years, with some skirmishes dating back to archaic times. First the Noxans would strike, and we Sylvanians would defend ourselves…and so it went back and forth until we adopted a treaty. The agreement lasted two years before the Noxans attacked again…and by this time, the Sylvanians were tired of fighting. They resorted to peaceful methods. They destroyed their own weapons and tried to talk things out with the Noxans.

That worked for a short while, but eventually the Noxans wouldn't have any of our peace talks and started attacking mercilessly. That's where the fourth hero of Vitreusia came in. She argued and debated tirelessly until the Sylvanians agreed to join Vitreusia and wage war upon the Noxans once more.

Under her leadership, the Noxans were driven back to their home world. Vitreusia and the Sylvanian Democracy were in contact for a millennium or so, with leaders visiting each other and joining forces when necessary, but gradually slipped out of touch over the last few hundred years.

A century or two before and after losing contact with Vitreusia, there were hardly any issues regarding the Noxans. There'd be a few sighted here, a small battle there, but nothing happened that was really monumental. Then the Sylvanian Democracy was sealed from the Republic of Noxa, and the issues all but disappeared."

Tahigwa shifted in his seat, and I could tell he was getting to the personal part of the story. "However, seven years ago, when my father held the president's office, Sylvania was attacked by the Noxans. How they breached the barrier, we still don't know today— but they assaulted us so quickly and in such large numbers it was nearly impossible to fight back.

I was only sixteen at the time. My father went out to talk with the leader of the Noxans, and they drew up a treaty. The next day the Noxans departed from Sylvania, and there was peace. For the next seven months, life was pretty much perfect. No war or fighting…just peace. Peace and quiet. Then one night…"

He shuddered, and a strange light shone through his green eyes: complete and utter horror. "I was lying in bed, in one of the bedrooms in this very house, when suddenly everything was dark. I couldn't see anything, not even my own hand in front of my face. The darkness coated me, chilling me to the bone. I felt my consciousness fading…and then I heard a scream that could only be my mother's.

My awareness rushed back as I jumped out of bed and groped my way to my parents' room. I blindly fumbled about the hallway for what seemed like an eternity…and then, unexpectedly, the darkness began to fade.

Able to see now, I ran all the way to my parents' bedroom. Upon coming in, I nearly fainted at the awful sight. Both my mother and father had been wounded. 'Tahigwa,' my mother sobbed, holding my father close, 'call a doctor, quickly!'

I ran and got a doctor, and when I returned, the look of death was on my father's face. The doctor rushed to his side. 'I don't think he'll make it,' he said after examining him.

He tended to both him and my mother, and while he bandaged my mother's wounds my father whispered, 'Tahigwa.'

I tore over to him, tears stinging my eyes. 'Yes, father.' 'I am dying. You must take my place as president.'

'No!'

'Tahigwa,' my father said, more kindly this time. 'It is your duty. Always remember…if someone is not of this world, they are not to be trusted. Not now, not ever. I leave Sylvania in your care. Be true to your name and make it at peace once more.'"

A couple of tears slid down Tahigwa's grey cheeks. "When he had said those words, he was only awake for a couple more minutes, and then he lost consciousness.

Early that morning..he passed away, and I became president, for in Sylvania when the president dies in office his oldest child takes up the task.

Though I haven't had many occasions to heed my father's advice, I have carried his dying words with me all these years. It's not much of an excuse, but I thought you should know." I swallowed, a lump in my throat and glanced over at Zach. His eyebrows went up as if to say, "Oh, man. What a story."

After a moment or two of silence, Aunt Leigh spoke up. "You didn't have to share this with us, but I appreciate you doing so...and although this is very late, I'm sorry for your loss."

Tahigwa nodded, and I could tell he was trying desperately to pull himself together. "Thank you. You're very kind." Aunt Leigh smiled compassionately (this is definitely not the first time I've noticed, but Aunt Leigh is extremely pretty).

Tahigwa arose from his seat, saying, "I'm sure this is a very important mission you're on. If we hurry, we can make it halfway through the Valley of Cheer before nightfall."

"Are you sure you want to come with us?" asked Aunt Leigh. "I hear it could be dangerous."

Tahigwa smiled ruefully, locking eyes with first Aunt Leigh, then Zach, then me. "Danger? I've lived in its shadow since I was born. And I'm more convinced that I should accompany you than I've ever been of anything in my life."

VIII.

Zach Easton

We walked along a narrow dirt path, following Tahigwa's lead. To be honest, I was still a little suspicious of the guy. After all, he had been extremely inhospitable upon finding us in the woods, and had even gone so far as to sentence Aunt Leigh to death! *"If she hadn't brought her dagger with her, there's no telling what would have happened to us,"* I thought to myself with a shudder.

As if she sensed my unrest, Leigh glanced in my direction, her grape-juice purple eyes questioning. I could practically hear her voice asking me: *"Is everything alright?"*

"Yes."

Leigh looked away, concentrating on the path before us. I lifted my head and took in the incredible sight of the Sylvanian sky. I had heard in social studies that it changed color and doubted it, but now, taking in the rainbow-hued sky, I saw. And I believed.

Tahigwa abruptly stopped walking, and I nearly bumped into my sister, who had gone in front of me while I gaped at the sky. He turned to face the three of us. "Be careful," he said. "It's very steep here." Upon beginning my descent I confirmed for myself that it indeed was very steep. Even Tahigwa, who had probably walked this path numerous times, wavered and came close to losing his balance on the incline which could almost be called a precipice.

Finally the hill flattened out, and we were walking on smooth ground.

"Friends," Tahigwa said in a whisper that conveyed great wonderment, "we are in the Valley of Cheer."

"It doesn't appear to be very cheerful.." remarked Leigh, glancing around at our surroundings. I scrutinized the area as well, and mutely agreed with my twin sister.

The place didn't look like a happy one. Sinister shadows were everywhere, and there was no color that I could see in the dim twilight.

Tahigwa shook his head. "No..this place is so named not for what you see, but for what you can't. Just silence your mouth and your mind...and listen." So we followed his advice.

At once a strange sensation washed over me. It was like my mind and spirit had received a breath of fresh air. Even though my brain was awash with a toxic mixture of emotions—fear, doubt, a smidge of anger...I suddenly felt at peace—content. I took a deep breath, letting this sensational feeling wash over me.

An eerie howl brought me back from my trance. I bit my tongue to keep from crying out, and Leigh shrieked. "What was that?" quavered Aunt Leigh.

Tahigwa had an air of indifference about him. Apparently this sort of thing was normal. "It was just a wolf spirit," he said calmly. "See?" He pointed to a wolf-like shape made out of light dashing across the sky.

"It's like the northern lights...only in the shape of a wolf," Aunt Leigh mused. "Incredible."

"I...would hope that they're not incredibly dangerous?" inquired Leigh.

Tahigwa laughed, the first time I had ever heard him do so. "Oh, no. They're completely harmless-and if you have fresh fish on hand, quite friendly."

"Huh," Leigh said to herself as we recommenced walking.

Aside from the howling of the wolf spirits, which occasionally took some or all of us off guard, the hike through the Valley of Cheer was rather uneventful. When Tahigwa announced that we had reached the halfway point and were going to camp out for the night, I felt pretty relieved. I hoped that the rest of the trip would be as easy as this walk in the park (pardon my awful attempt at making a joke).

As I made myself comfortable upon my moss bed (a natural part of the valley, surprisingly), the feeling of comfort left me. The fear of having another unsettling nightmare kept me awake, while the others were all fast asleep, worn out from the day's adventures.

The sky had just turned a deep shade of indigo, and I was finally beginning to grow sleepy when a sudden movement made me sit up in alarm. There, standing not five feet away from where I sat, was the very same Noxan I'd seen in the book!

Everything about her was exactly the same, from the unique way her hair was braided in a sort of headband around her head to her eyes, which were dark, deep pools of blackness. Her smooth, caramel-colored skin shone in the wolf spirits' milky light. She studied me for a brief moment, then thrust her hands out towards me. An inky mist came swirling from them and began to enclose me in a shroud of darkness. "No, this can't happen again!" I thought in protest. "How can I fight this?"

My father's words came back to me. The Noxans were the people of dark and the night…and night eventually gave way to day, and dark was dispelled by light.

"Light," I realized. *"I need light."* An ancient instinct took over within me, and I kept thinking that word over and over. *"Light. Lucem."* I had thought the word several times when I started to feel warm. Very warm.

My body began to emit a golden-yellow light—much brighter than my natural Vitreusian aura. I felt warmer and warmer, and I glowed brighter and brighter. Then the wind was knocked out of me by the most powerful energy wave I had ever felt. The darkness left me, and I stopped glowing. For a little more than thirty seconds, I lay on the ground, gasping for air.

When I had the strength to sit up again, *she* was still there. Apparently the energy wave had hit her hard, too, for she was breathing heavily and her forehead glistened with beads of sweat. "No…" she murmured, so softly I had to strain to hear her. "Suus 'impossibile." Then she looked up and saw that I was sitting up.

"You…are stronger than most."

I raised an eyebrow. "Who are you?"

She stood up, brushing herself off. "My name is Zynthia Avariss, of the Republic of Noxa," she said, a mysterious edge to her voice. The color of her eyes changed from black to a bright, fiery orange. "And you, Vitreusian,"—she scowled as the name of my homeland fell from her lips—"never saw me." And with a wave of her hand she was gone.

IX.

Leigh Kline

Early the next morning, we all got up—except for Zach, that is. He slept soundly while we got ready for the day of hiking ahead of us.

After about five minutes, everything being ready, Leigh shook him awake. His eyes opened, and Leigh cried out in surprise. Tahigwa gasped. His normally purple eyes were all black! Then he blinked groggily, and the mist, as it was, cleared away. Seeing our startled faces, he asked confusedly, "What's wrong?"

"Your eyes…" Leigh said, her voice wavering. "They were completely black!" A flash of recognition appeared in Zach's purple eyes, there one moment, gone the next. Leigh's purple eyes narrowed in suspicion, and she locked eyes with Zach, giving him a questioning look.

Austin and Christina had told me that the twins had a

special connection, being able to communicate with each other on an almost telepathic level. However, if Zach knew anything about what had just happened, he wasn't telling, for Leigh turned away, the expression on her face a mixture of puzzlement and hurt. She gave him one last pained glance and then rose. "We should get going," she said in the gruff tone she used when she was upset.

Tahigwa's countenance was a combination of bewilderment and concern. He opened his mouth to say something, but I shook my head at him and he immediately swallowed whatever he was going to say. Clearing his throat, he started over: "We'd better get going. It's best to climb Courage Mountain in the daytime hours."

He began to lead us through the valley once more, and Zach slipped past Leigh and I to walk with Tahigwa. I whispered as softly as possible to Leigh: "What's wrong with Zach?"

She turned to me, and the fear in her eyes was as plain as day. "I don't know. He's shutting me out…he never does that, not even when he's really mad at me. Ever since we were little, it was like our minds were sort of…bridged together, you know? All these years, all he and I have ever had to do to communicate was simply walk across that 'bridge'."

"And now?" I prompted.

Leigh took a deep breath. "He…he destroyed it, Aunt Leigh. On purpose. For some reason, he doesn't want me to cross it anymore, and now…I can't even ask him why."

"You could speak aloud to him…" I suggested.

Leigh shook her head. "No…that wouldn't work."

"How do you know that?"

She knit her azure eyebrows. "I…I just know. I've always known these sorts of things with him. I've learned to trust those instincts."

I nodded, and we fell into silence, following Tahigwa's lead.

While watching out for thorns and holes, among other things, I kept a close eye on Zach. He and Tahigwa talked briefly, but they quickly dropped back into an awkward quiet. I observed that Zach seemed very out of it. His eyes had returned to their normal shade of deep purple, but it was as if a mist was still over them—figuratively speaking. He tripped over rocks, stumbled into brambles, and even bumped into a tree. Every time he did one of these things, Leigh winced, as if the way he stumbled about hurt her, too.

Suddenly, Tahigwa halted in his tracks and turned around, Zach turning with him. "We're almost there," the leader of the Sylvanian Democracy said, making eye contact with first Leigh, then me. Zach's face was blank as he locked eyes with Leigh. They held each other's gaze for a little less than thirty seconds, and then Tahigwa turned and started to walk once more.

"Is he still blocking you?" I inquired of Leigh softly.

She turned a mournful pair of purple eyes upon me. "Yes. I asked him what was wrong…and he said, 'I can't tell you Leigh. Not you, not anybody. I have to keep this to myself, deal with this alone. Please don't take it personally.'"

I swallowed hard. *"This is not good,"* I thought to myself. *"Who knows what he's hiding? And if Leigh can't find out what it is, **nobody** can."*

Aloud I said, "he'll open up about it eventually—to you at least." I spoke confidently, and Leigh appeared to be reassured somewhat.

My own mind, however, was engulfed in a swirling maelstrom of frightening theories. Perhaps Zach had another bad dream the previous night, and he knew now that Zach—my friend Zach—has slipped under…for good.

Tahigwa spoke, startling me out of my worrisome speculations. "There it is," he said, with an undertone of awe. "Courage Mountain."

X.

Leigh Hollis

I looked up at the tallest mountain I'd ever seen in my
life. I'd thought Glass Mountain back home was
pretty darn lofty, but *this?* Try three Glass Mountains
stacked on top of each other. As if the sheer height of
the thing wasn't daunting enough, fires blazed on
various parts of the mountain, and overgrown
thickets of thorns stood silhouetted against the now
blood-red Sylvanian sky. Winged creatures circled
both the mountain's peak and the area several feet
below it.

I will admit that I pride myself on my courage, but
this? This struck a good amount of fear into my heart.
I stole a cautious glance at Zach. His face had turned
deathly pale, and his knees were knocking about
slightly—just enough for me to notice (which didn't
take much at all, really—I did live with him, after all).
Aunt Leigh was struggling to keep a brave expression

on her face—probably more for our sake than for hers or Tahigwa's.

Speaking of Tahigwa, even he looked unsettled. That was what bothered me the most about this situation. I made eye contact with Zach, begging him to open up to me again. *"Please, Zach. Don't shut me out like this."*

His features were grim and apologetic as he answered without a word: *"I don't have much choice."* I snapped back in reply: *"You always have a choice!"*

He responded: *"I'm trying to protect you."*

I gritted my teeth. Was he *trying* to make me mad? *"You don't have to protect me! We can solve this together, like we always have! Heck, when we were little and you were terrified of the dark we shared a room! We've always been able to work things out! Why is now any different??"*

He dropped his eyes—those intense purple eyes, exact replicas of my own—and answered: *"This darkness is different. It is powerful, intense-almost impossible to stop."*

I clapped my hand over my mouth to keep from saying something out loud. *"You've been attacked by a Noxan, haven't you?"*

The connection between our minds began to fade. Zach was shutting me out again. *"Zach, stop!"* I pleaded. *"Don't lock me out! Please!"*

I could see a tear beginning to form in Zach's eye. *"I've said too much already,"* he responded, and even though the words weren't spoken I could sense the sorrow and the pain pulsing through them.

"No! Don't do this to me!!" But he had already

severed the tie.

Overcome by my heartache, I dropped to one knee. I did my best to restrain my tears as Aunt Leigh and Tahigwa concernedly asked what was wrong. "It's Zach," I choked, and though Tahigwa looked confused, Aunt Leigh understood immediately.

She helped me to my feet and inquired of Tahigwa: "Do we have to go to the top of this mountain?"

Tahigwa closed his eyes, thinking hard. "If I remember correctly," he said slowly, "it is not required to go to the top, but rather, halfway and through the natural tunnel in the center of the mountain."

"I see," Aunt Leigh said seriously, watching me with a worried glint in her blue eyes.

Tahigwa nodded, and began to wave his hands in a twisting motion, creating a long vine. As he did this he said, "I must warn you about this place. It is the ultimate test of valor. I could tell that you thought the fire, the thorns, and the winged gazelles were startling…well, truthfully speaking, you haven't seen anything yet. Climbing this mountain, you will see everything that you—and you alone—are most afraid of. You won't see everything at once, but I assure you, by the end of this climb you will have seen every one of your greatest fears.

However, if you keep one thing in mind, you'll likely make it down the mountain with your sanity. The images and personages which you will see cannot harm you in any way. The thorns and fires, yes, but your fears are made out of mist, and nothing more. As hard as it will be, to make the illusion vanish, you must walk towards it and through it. Then it will vanish. Do you understand?"

I nodded yes, biting my lip. I was both dreading the climb and looking forward to finishing it at the same time. Tahigwa looked from face to face, making sure we comprehended his advice and warnings.

"Well," he said with a deep inhalation (needless to say, he wasn't anticipating the ascension of Courage Mountain, either). "I've got the rope, so we might as well get this over with."

◆ ◆ ◆

Tahigwa hurled the rope upwards at the mountain, lassoing a jagged rock. He weaved four more ropes, approximately two feet long, and gave one to each of us, keeping one for himself. "Tie it to your hand, and then I'll tie it to the main rope," he said.

We did as he requested, and Zach spoke up. "What purpose does this serve?"

"It's to make sure we stick together."

"Why wouldn't we?" Zach pressed.

Tahigwa shook his head knowingly. "This is my reaction to these apparitions, and perhaps the three of you may respond differently, but I wanted to run…just run. I wanted to sprint away from those images, away from everything. Had I not been tied in the same manner which we will be, I would probably be living on this mountain now—a haunted shell of a person." He shuddered.

Zach did not ask any more questions, and remained silent while Tahigwa knotted our ropes to the main rope in such a way that they were secure but could still slide up and down as we climbed. He walked to the front of us and tied his rope as well. Tahigwa inhaled deeply in an obvious attempt to calm his nerves. I knew that whatever he had seen up here, however long ago he had seen it, still haunted him.

He turned to face us, and I noticed a pallor spreading through his grey complexion. "Well," he said, "the hike up to the cave where we'll spend the night shouldn't take very long—about until purple skies. Let's go."

He began to ascend the mountain, grasping the rope for support. Aunt Leigh went next, Zach after her, and I was the last one to start climbing. I had taken no more than ten steps when Tahigwa vanished into the thick fog up ahead.

A few minutes later, I also stepped into that cold, moist shroud of white, bracing myself for whatever I might see. At first, I did not perceive anything frightening. *"Maybe this won't be as bad as Tahigwa said it would be,"* I thought hopefully to myself.

I climbed some more and then saw something out of the corner of my eye. Given what Tahigwa had told us about this place, I should have turned away and concentrated on scaling the mountain. My curiosity got the better of me, though, so I turned to see what it was. *Vitreusia.*

My homeland was projected right before my eyes, in all its uncomplicated beauty. The view was unchanged for a few seconds, and then something began to happen. Something terrible.

A dark mist came swirling over the land—from where it came I couldn't tell—and began to cloak everything in blackness.

It all started to fade—the hospital, the houses…everything. I could hear shouts and cheers—*Noxans*. Thousands of voices began reciting the battle cry of the Noxans—*Grando omnem tenebris! All hail the dark!*

I covered my eyes, turned and tried to run—but the rope on my wrist yanked me back. The quick, sharp pain of the rope cutting into my wrist brought me back to my senses, and though it was the last thing I wanted to do, I walked towards and through that frightening image. Tahigwa's advice worked: as soon as I did that, the mirage vanished.

With a sigh of relief I walked back over to the rope and recommenced the ascent. I was pretty lonely, as the fog hid my companions from sight, so I was glad when I was able to see Zach ahead of me.

Looking up from finding a suitable foothold, I realized he was watching me—and that his eyes had turned black. Horror pierced my chest.

"Zach!" I half shouted, half screamed.

"I'm afraid it's too late, Leigh," he said emptily, the blackness washing over every part of him—his hair, his skin, *everything.*

"No!" I cried, running towards him as fast as I could. His knees began to shake, and he crumpled to the ground. I had just reached his side…and then he disappeared. I gasped for air, my heart threatening to burst right out of my rib cage. The whole thing had been a hallucination. Breathing a quick sigh of relief, I initiated my hike once more.

Several upsetting apparitions later, we were reunited in the natural tunnel which Tahigwa had mentioned earlier. Looking around at everyone, they all had the same look to them: ashen, disheveled, and frightened. Although I had no idea what they had seen, I wasn't about to ask. I had enough nightmarish images in my head from my own journey.

We sat there, not too close together, not too far apart. Nobody spoke. The only sound was that of our own heavy, ragged breathing. We avoided eye contact with each other, as if afraid we could glimpse the horrors our cohorts had seen by looking into their eyes. And things stayed this way for a rather lengthy amount of time.

XI.

Zach Easton

Tahigwa broke the uncomfortable silence. "We must cease thinking of the things we saw climbing this mountain before there is permanent damage," he said, rummaging through his satchel.

"Like permanent damage hasn't been done already," Leigh muttered, winding her azure tresses around her fingers.

Tahigwa sighed empathetically. "I will admit the images I took in on my first climb up this mountain still trouble me…but only from time to time. After scaling this mountain, you must distract yourself. Otherwise those mirages will consume you."

"And how am I supposed to do this?" inquired Leigh.

Tahigwa smiled knowingly. "I will show you—all of you." I raised an eyebrow as he pulled thin rectangles of wood and a couple of sticks with notches on them out of his bag.

"Come in a little closer," he said. "We can't be too far apart for this."

"And may I ask what *this* is?" Leigh said as she followed Tahigwa's instructions.

"Ludnum," replied Tahigwa, handing us each three wood rectangles. "It's probably unfamiliar to you three, as it's only played in the Sylvanian Democracy. As a matter of fact, it is a very simple game, and I am going to teach it to all of you."

He gave us each three pieces of wood, and gave himself three as well. He set the sticks on the ground and said: "Now, everybody pick up your cards." We did as he requested. "I'll go first so you all know what to do." He picked up the sticks and let them roll off his fingertips.

When they stopped rolling he said, "Notice how many notches are left face-up on the sticks—three in this case. That means I pick up three cards. I can keep a maximum of four."

He switched out the cards, discarding four of them and putting them in a separate pile. "The goal is to have three of the same kind," he said. "If you get three of a kind, throw down your cards. You will win that round, and we'll go on to the next one.

Seven is the number of rounds to be traditionally played, with more or less being acceptable, as long as the number of rounds is not divisible by the number of players. We'll play seven rounds, if that's alright with all of you."

"Fine with me," Aunt Leigh said.

"I'm game," Leigh said.

I shrugged.

The game began. I had a pair in my hand when Leigh threw down her cards triumphantly. "Fast learner!" Tahigwa remarked approvingly. "This will be a very competitive game."

Aunt Leigh frowned as she drew and discarded her cards...only to slap them down upon the floor the next instant. She observed my surprised expression and laughed softly. I couldn't help but smile back at her. I took the next round, and Leigh the one after that.

"I've been playing this game for years, yet I am the one who has not won a single round yet!" Tahigwa remarked smilingly as he dealt the cards out for the fifth round.

Ironically enough, Tahigwa won both that round and the following round. "I wonder if Leigh or I will win…" he mused as we studied our cards. "..or perhaps there will be a three-way tie." Leigh smiled slightly, a competitive gleam in her eyes.

We all stole wary glances at each other, seeing if we could read each other's expressions (to see if they looked like they might be close to winning, that is).

Aunt Leigh's face was serious, but she had proven to us in a previous round that she could hide her emotions (as far as the game went, at least).

Leigh's eyebrows were close together as she studied her cards. Then she let out a sigh.

"What is it?" I asked aloud.

She grinned and threw down her cards. "I just won," she said with an air of mock smugness.

"Excellent work, Leigh," Tahigwa said.

"Thanks." She blushed. "It's really a game of luck, though, isn't it?"

"Half luck, half strategy—as my father said when he first taught me how to play," Tahigwa replied.

He proceeded to create a pile of kindling and start a fire. He handed each of us a small pillow and an intricately woven blanket.

We all stretched out upon the floor of the cave, which (luckily) was quite mossy and therefore not intolerably hard. The other three were soon asleep, and soon the only sound to be heard within the cave was the crackling and popping of the fire.

I was actually rather tired, but what I had seen on my climb up the mountain still disturbed me—and very much so.

As I rolled over for what seemed like the four hundredth time, I saw a slender yet muscular figure sitting by the fire. I immediately recognized the black hair and the unique way it was styled, the dark mist emitting from her bronzed skin. *"You,"* I said in an accusatory tone.

She jumped, startled, and turned to face me. "You are not pleased to see me," she stated, her black eyes boring into me.

I scoffed. "Is there any reason why I would be?"

She turned away from me and watched the orange tongues of fire licking away at the wood. "I could have killed you, you know," she said softly.

I bit back heated words. "If you were capable of it then why didn't you?"

She coughed into her elbow. "You…remind me of someone."

"Someone?" I repeated dubiously. "That was their name? Someone?"

She whirled to face me, her eyes glowing a bright orange. "You *dare* to mock me, Vitreusian?" she said in a threatening tone, a ball of black mist swirling in her left hand.

"Easy, Zynthia," I said as calmly as I could, considering the circumstances. "I'm curious as to who this person is."

"Is?" she said, turning her back on me. "You mean *was.*"

I did not pursue that topic any further. It was clear that it was a sensitive one. Besides, I had no desire to be cloaked in darkness.

"Why are you here?" I asked.

"I am not going to tell you, **Vitreusian.**"

I winced. She said *Vitreusian* in the way you might say *serial killer* or *racist*.

"Why do you say it like that?!" I exclaimed.

She turned, her eyes now a striking blue-green. "Say what like that?"

"Vitreusian. You let it plummet from your tongue like a curse! Why?"

She exhaled, quickly and hard. "Has no one told you yet? You are certainly old enough to know."

"Know what?" She shook her head in disbelief. "What? Tell me!"

She waved her hand dismissively, a stream of darkness swirling from it and making curlicues in the dimly lit cave. "I would never spew hatred towards my homeland, my race."

"*What?*"

"Ask your companions. *They* will tell you."

"No, I want *you* to tell me."

"Why would I care what you want?" she retorted, standing up. "Be forewarned. The next time we meet, I might not be so gracious."

"*Gracious?*" I echoed. but she was already gone.

XII.

Leigh Kline

When I awoke, the fire had gone out, and Leigh was up, but Tahigwa and Zach were still fast asleep on the cave floor.

"Bonum mane," Leigh said.

"Bonum mane," I replied, getting up and stretching. "Sleep well?" I asked.

She made a wry face. "Eh...not too badly."

"Same here."

Just then Tahigwa stirred and set eyes upon the two of us. "Good morning, Leighs," he said with a smile.

"Good morning," we replied.

"Please tell me we don't have to go through that...dreadfulness on the way down, too," Leigh said, her voice trembling.

Tahigwa shook his head vigorously. "Thankfully, no. The way down is much less traumatic than the climb up.”

Leigh breathed a sigh of relief.

“Wait!” cried Zach, startling us all. “Don’t go…”

Leigh’s purple eyes opened wide. She rushed over to where her brother tossed and turned.

“Zynthia, stop!” he said, more softly this time.

Leigh swallowed hard and started to shake him gently. “Wake up, Zach!”

His eyelids popped open. “Lucem!” he cried, and a sphere of light whirled in his hand.

“Zach, it’s *me!*” The orb disappeared as quickly as it had materialized.

“I’m sorry, Leigh,” he said. “I was having a…rather unpleasant dream.”

“I managed to deduce that,” Leigh rejoined coolly. “What was that little trick?”

“Trick?” Zach seemed confused.

“Yeah, trick. The globe of light you summoned upon waking up.”

“It was all instinct, I swear,” he answered.

“And who did you think I was? You’d never attack me, and even if you did, you couldn’t do it with light.” Before Zach could say a word Leigh burst out, “Don’t make up anything! You thought I was a Noxan, didn’t you?”

Zach did not reply.

Leigh’s voice rose several octaves as she went on, “What *are* you up to? Whatever it is, it can’t be any good.”

“I—” Zach began, but Leigh cut him off once more.

"You can only hide this from me for so long, Zach. Either you tell me, or I'll find out," she said in a threatening tone.

Tahigwa cleared his throat. "Let's not waste time arguing. The faster we get through that forest, the better."

Leigh swallowed. "What horrors await us there?"

Tahigwa shook his head. "The Forest of Ethereality is nothing compared to Courage Mountain."

"What goes on in there?" Zach asked cautiously.

"You'll hear voices from your past—the good, the bad, and everything in between. Another thing: do *not* stray from the paths. If you do, you could stumble across a portal...and once you go through one of those, you'll probably never make it back to your own time and place."

Leigh grimaced. "I certainly won't do any exploring. Not that I was planning to, anyway."

"Well!" Tahigwa said, throwing his satchel over his shoulder. "Shall we go?" We all nodded.

◆ ◆ ◆

Standing at the edge of the other side of the tunnel, I looked down at the swirling mist that concealed how high up we were. My heart was in my throat as I inquired of Tahigwa: "Are you *sure* that we're supposed to jump?"

"Yeah..." Zach agreed. "I really, really, *really* don't like this." Leigh nodded slightly to show that she was likeminded.

"I'm certain," Tahigwa answered. "It's the way

which must be taken. This is Courage Mountain, after all. Even the easiest route isn't all that effortless."

"So, we have to jump," Leigh said, pursing her lips.

"Yes," Tahigwa replied.

"Into that swirling abyss of mist, which is covering up who-knows-what?"

"Everything will be fine," he assured her. "I promise." Leigh closed her eyes and, taking a deep breath, leapt off the precipice. Tahigwa followed suit, and Zach and I jumped off as well.

Down I plunged into the cold, wet mist, which hid my companions from view. I compared the sensation to a roller coaster—except that there wasn't a track, or a train. I was just falling.

Just as I started to think that I would never reach solid ground, I began to decelerate, and I was slowly lowered down onto soft grass. A gust of wind blew away all the fog in one blast, and I could now see that my friends had reached the ground as well.

"W—well…" Leigh quavered, her features pale. "That was…exhilarating."

Tahigwa chuckled. "A distinctive way of putting it, Leigh."

Leigh smiled shyly and tugged at a strand of her azure hair.

"So…" said Zach, somewhat awkwardly, "I assume *that* over there is the Forest of Ethereality?" He pointed to what, if you took away the fact that the trees were purple and silver and glittered as if stardust had been painted on them, looked like a dense forest.

Tahigwa nodded in affirmation. "Yes indeed. A beautiful, mysterious place, that. We should move through it quickly, however," He made eye contact with each of us before explaining, "I cannot leave my people for long…not with a Noxan prowling about."

"Oh…that's right," Leigh said.

"Let's go," Tahigwa said, heading for the woods.

Once inside, I began to hear voices, murmuring and whispering things which I couldn't make out. Then, as I got further in, the voices became clearer.

"I love you, Leigh," spoke my mom's voice. Shortly afterwards, a harsh laugh echoed in my ears.

"I'm not even your *friend*-let alone your *best* friend." I swallowed. *Adrienne.*

I stole a glance at first Leigh, then Zach. Their faces changed from happy to upset to angry as they heard snatches of past memories.

Tahigwa's back was to me, and he studied the ground carefully as he ambled along, making sure we were following the right path. The voices kept coming. Some sentences had been spoken years ago. Others were fairly new in the timeline of my life.

"This is not the Vitreusia I left," Christina's voice whispered.

"The time has come for you to make a difficult choice," said a voice which I recognized as Austin's.

Then I heard Tahigwa say, "Almost there."

I snapped out of my near-trance. "Tahigwa? Did you actually say that?"

He stopped and turned around, making eye contact with me. "Yes, I did. We'll be out in a matter of minutes."

"How odd," I thought but didn't say. *"I feel as if we've been wandering through this forest for ten minutes at most."*

As if he'd read my mind, Tahigwa added: "The forest distorts your sense of time while you're in it, but once we're out, the so-called fog will clear away from our minds."

"Thank you for explaining that to me," I said in a tone of gratitude. He nodded and went back to leading us.

It felt like an hour had passed when Tahigwa began to exit the forest, Leigh following him. I was bringing up the rear.

I heard one more voice before I stepped out of that strange forest: Zach's. "Leigh, go!"

My hand flew up to my forehead. I felt like I'd been stabbed in the chest.

"Are you okay, Aunt Leigh?" Leigh asked concernedly as she took a swig of water.

"I'm fine," I answered.

"Okay…" she replied. "Hey, what's that?" she said all of a sudden, pointing to a tree off in the distance.

"The Tree of Vitality," Tahigwa responded.

"Let's go!" Zach exclaimed. but before we could take a single step towards that tree, a dark mist swept in front of us.

When it cleared, a girl was standing there. She was tall and toned, with olive skin and black eyes. Her hair was black, and her face, although very pretty, was serious.

"Stay where you are," she said in a commanding manner. "Do what I say, and maybe you won't get hurt."

"*Excuse me?*" Leigh snapped. "Who do you think you are?"

The girl's eyes changed colors, from an inky black to a bright orange. "I am Zynthia Avariss, of the Republic of Noxa."

"Well, *Zynthia,*" Leigh said, her purple eyes snapping with fury, "I for one will not take orders from you."

Zynthia's eyes were now a fiery red, the color of hot coals. "Fine then." She spoke a single word in a low voice, and a sphere of dark mist began to swirl in her hand.

Zach, who had been quiet ever since Zynthia had appeared, spoke up. "Zynthia, stop!" She looked up, her eyes changing to a teal shade. "You can't do this. We can work this out!"

The teal faded into grey, then yellow. "Clearly you haven't studied any history," she said, preparing to throw her ball of darkness.

"You leave me no choice!" Zach cried. *"Lucem!"* An orb of light appeared in his left palm.

He locked eyes with Leigh for one, two seconds, and then they turned to Tahigwa and I and said simultaneously, "Go! We'll hold her off!"

I froze, torn. The Tree of Vitality was only a couple of minutes' run away. Once I got the sap, I would be one big step closer to reviving Zach. but this Noxan was powerful—she had to be to breach the Sylvanian Democracy's barriers. Leigh and Zach might not be able to hold their own...and I would never forgive myself if anything happened to either of them.

Tahigwa studied the twins closely, and his eyes grew large, as if he were remembering something—something important.

"Twins..." he murmured to himself. "Equally powerful in the ways of light..." I opened my mouth to ask what he meant, but he unknowingly cut me short, saying, "They'll be fine. To the tree!" He took off, and I ran to keep up with him.

When we reached the tree, a man appeared out of thin air. He was short and muscular, with skin a shade lighter than Tahiwga's and the same vibrant green eyes and hair.

"I am the keeper of the Tree of Vitality," he said without the slightest trace of emotion. "No one touches a drop of its sap without my consent."

"Well," I said, "May we have your permission, then? Please?"

"Who is the sap for?"

"My friend, Zach. He was killed years ago—well not exactly, he's an inter duos, but he's caught between life and death and I must save him!"

"You do not convince me," he replied in the same stolid voice.

"Please!" I looked over my shoulder at where Zach and Leigh clashed with the Noxan. Leigh and Zach glowed with the warm, golden-yellow light unique to Vitreusians. Zynthia Avariss' tall figure emitted a dark mist. All three of their auras were weakening.

"Our friends don't have much time. We beseech you to give us some of the sap, please!" Tahiwga entreated.

"I am not moved," he answered. I was about to make my reply when a very loud sound filled my ears. I likened it to a firework, echoing out over mountains. I whirled around, and Zynthia, Zach, and Leigh all lay motionless on the ground.

I began to choke up as I turned to face the keeper. "I lost my best friend years and years ago. Every day between then and now has been more or less a struggle. And those twins...they helped me! They helped me cope with the memory of my friend being gunned down by a horrible FBI agent! They helped me put the past out of my mind, even though I still have nightmares about it! They risked their lives to come here on this mission to bring my friend back to life!"

Tears were flowing down my face now. "Have you no empathy, no compassion!? These two and their parents gave me *hope!* A reason to wake up and see the sun rising and say, 'It is good to be alive!'"

"I have heard enough!" the keeper shouted. An axe materialized in his hand. I reached for my dagger, but I had wrongly guessed his intentions. He swung the axe at the tree, making a huge gash in its trunk. A small crystal vial appeared beside him, and he picked it up and collected the blue, glittering sap which had begun to flow from the tree.

He closed up the bottle and waved his hand at the tree. The gash vanished. "Take this," he said, handing me the crystal vial. "You have more than earned it." I took the vial, and both the keeper and the tree shimmered—and vanished.

Tahigwa and I glanced at each other and ran towards where the twins lay on the ground. They were still insensible. The Noxan hadn't begun to rouse yet either. Tahiwga rushed over to Leigh, I to Zach.

"She's breathing," he reported.

"Zach is too."

"What about the Noxan—Zynthia?"

I sucked in my cheeks. "Should I check?"

"I don't know if that's a good idea." Just then Zach's eyelids began to flutter. "He's about to come to."

"Same thing over here," Tahigwa answered, his eyes on Leigh.

Zach sat up. "Where's Zynthia?" were the first words out of his mouth.

"Over there," I said, pointing to where she lay unconscious.

Zach looked around him in a panic. "Where's Leigh?"

"Right over there."

She was also sitting up now, her freckled face both confused and angry. "Are you okay?" she called to Zach.

"Yes. You?"

"I'm fine!" she answered. Slowly, the twins got up.

Zynthia began to stir. "Oh…" she moaned. Then she saw the four of us and scrambled to her feet. "You have not seen the last of me!" she cried, enveloping herself in darkness and fleeing across the countryside.

Leigh sighed. "Mom and Dad were right about the Noxans. They really are an outlandish race."

Zach flashed Leigh a silent message with his purple eyes, and Leigh seemed to respond wordlessly.

"Did you get the sap?" Zach asked. A triumphant smile began to spread across my face. I had nearly forgotten the sap in my concern for the twins.

"Yes. Let me get the book…"

A moment later I had retrieved it from my satchel and opened it to the page where we were supposed to place a drop of the sap. Handling the vial with the utmost care, I dispensed a tiny drop of the blue, sparkly sap onto the paper.

The drop shimmered and vanished. I held my breath as traces of Vitreusian calligraphy began to appear on the page…

XIII.

Leigh Hollis

Aunt Leigh handed the primeval book to me with trembling hands. "Read this, Leigh, please," she said.

"I'll do my best," I answered, squinting at the elaborate script. *"The trouble has all but ended, your journey nearly through. Find where the one you seek to wake was most alive. Then on the ground, slowly write their name with the sap you took such pains to obtain. Breathe upon that name, and then-the one who has been lost will find their way again."*

"Is that all?" Aunt Leigh inquired.

"Yes."

After pondering this a bit she said, "Well, I have a few ideas as to where this place could be, and they're all in Vitreusia."

"I can call a wolf spirit for you to take you back to your land," Tahigwa volunteered.

"Would you like to come with us?" Zach asked.

"Would I like to? Yes, I would, very much. However, I am the president of a nation—and a nation which is threatened by the darkest of adversaries. Leaving my world would be quite negligent of me."

"I understand completely, Tahigwa," Aunt Leigh responded.

"I thank you very much for your help. I doubt we would have succeeded without you."

"I'm sure an intelligent and resourceful trio like you would have found a way."

My cheeks suddenly felt hot, and I rubbed them in an attempt to cool them down. Thankfully, Tahigwa did not notice my sudden awkwardness, for he was busy fashioning a wooden whistle, which he blew once completed. Eerie howls filled the air, and three wolf spirits soon were in front of us.

"Uhm, pardon my ignorance," I began, "but seeing as they're *spirits,* how are we supposed to, you know, ride on them or whatever?"

Tahigwa smiled, warmth spreading through his handsome features. My cheeks started to get hot again. "An astute observation, Leigh. You sort of step *into* them..and you'll be transported swiftly and safely to Vitreusia."

"Like this?" Zach inquired before he was swallowed up by the intense light of the wolf spirit. I gasped.

"Don't worry. He'll be fine." Tahigwa reassured Aunt Leigh and me.

"Thank you again," Aunt Leigh said, stepping into another wolf spirit.

"My pleasure," Tahigwa replied just before she disappeared in a swirl of stardust.

As it sunk in that Tahigwa and I were now alone, I felt that stupid burning upon my cheeks. "I guess I should go," I said, sidling towards the remaining wolf spirit. "It was nice meeting you."

"It was a pleasure to meet you as well, Leigh," he answered, extending his hand.

As we shook hands, I felt something rough and kind of lumpy. I thought nothing of it, for his skin had a texture similar to tree bark, but when I withdrew my hand, I found an intricately woven bracelet, which changed colors as I turned it over in my hand—green, orange, yellow, red, brown, and back to green again.

I looked up at Tahigwa inquiringly.

"Just so you'll remember me," he said with a small wink.

"It's beautiful. Thank you."

He merely smiled. I put the bracelet on my left wrist and stepped into the wolf spirit.

"I'll remember," I promised him before he, and all of the Sylvanian Democracy, vanished before my eyes.

◆ ◆ ◆

The journey between worlds was magnificent, although a bit frightening at first. For a moment or two, everything was dark. Then I felt cold air on my face, as if I were moving very fast. When my hair momentarily blew out of my face I saw white light streaking by in smooth lines.

The whole thing lasted for less than fifteen

seconds, at the end of which I found myself standing on the hill that overlooked Vitreusia's main community.

Aunt Leigh and Zach were close by. They looked greatly relieved. "We were afraid something had happened," Aunt Leigh explained.

"I'm fine. Where do you think this place is? Where—um—Zach (since I had never met him, nor discussed him with anyone often, I was at a total loss as to what to call him) was most alive?"

Aunt Leigh nodded. "Yes. I think we will head to the keeper of the necklace and dagger's hut first."

We made our way down to the village, trying not to draw attention to ourselves. The bluish purple glitter which covered all three of us (I assumed it was stardust or something to that effect), though, caused our fellow villagers to stare at us curiously.

I was relieved when Aunt Leigh stopped at the hut, which was closed up—it had been for as long as I could remember, since Zach was dead and Aunt Leigh, the twenty-third Salvator, was still living.

Aunt Leigh knelt down on the little stoop and wrote my brother's namesake's full name with her sap-covered index finger in a cautious way, as if the slightest mistake would void the revival. *Zach Dean Johnston.*

Leaning down close to the writing, she breathed upon it and stood back. Nothing happened. The sap merely sparkled in the afternoon light. Then, the writing peeled off the ground and twirled up to the sky in a glittery tornado. After that, nothing else happened.

"I guess that wasn't the right spot," Aunt Leigh said.

"I guess not," Zach said solemnly.

"Where else could it be?" I asked.

"Maybe…maybe in the gorge—" Aunt Leigh cut herself off. "No. No. It couldn't be there."

Zach turned to me, an anxious glimmer in his eyes. *This doesn't look good. What if we can't find this place, or run out of sap?"*

I bit my lip. The thought had occurred to me as well. *"We'll find it,"* I told him.

"I hope so."

"Aunt Leigh," I said aloud, "you knew my brother's namesake very well. Was there perhaps a place in Vitreusia that was very special to him? A cave, maybe? Or a valley? Perhaps the orchard near the gorge?"

Aunt Leigh's eyes lit up. "That's it!" she exclaimed. "Glass Mountain!" She broke into a run towards the iridescent peak.

Zach and I looked at each other and sprinted to catch up.

One hard climb, two water breaks and several near curse-words later, the three of us were on the ledge on Glass Mountain which was close to its peak.

"This has to be it," Aunt Leigh murmured to herself as she knelt down to write. She formed each letter, carefully, lovingly, until at last the name of *Zach Dean Johnston* glittered upon the ground once more.

Leaning in close to the writing, she exhaled, and

then took a couple steps back. The name began to glow, brighter and brighter.

When I had just about been blinded, all three names were lifted from the ground and swirled into a shimmering vortex. Faster and faster it churned. The sap began to take on a shape—the silhouette of a tall, slender man.

Suddenly Zach breathed in sharply and pointed to the feet of the figure. *Sneakers.* Cerulean ones, with bright green laces.

The rest began to fill in. Khaki pants. A black t-shirt that said: **Stop bullying.**

I got my first glimpse of Zach's face. His hair was light brown and neatly combed. His eyes were closed, so I couldn't tell what color they were. I glanced at Aunt Leigh. She looked like she might be in a state of shock.

The sap, now encircling my brother's namesake, hurled itself at Zach's body, spreading all over him. *His eyes—striking hazel eyes—opened.*

His chest puffed out as he took the first breath he'd taken in years. His eyes settled on Aunt Leigh.

"Leigh…you did it," he said in a weak voice.

"Zach…" Aunt Leigh breathed, rushing to his side, supporting him as he tried to walk. "He's..very ill.." Aunt Leigh said, her breath coming in ragged gasps. "We must get him to the hospital—and quickly."

XIV.

Zach Easton

The next week-and-a-half or so was utterly chaotic.
Naturally, the whole of Vitreusia was filled with great
jubilation at the return of its esteemed hero.
However, my namesake was very sick. Aunt Leigh
was constantly at his bedside, tending to his every
need. For awhile, my sister and I feared he would not
make it.

One day, Aunt Leigh woke up at dawn and headed
for the room where my namesake had been for the
last few days. She found him making his bed.
Apparently he had made a near full recovery
overnight. The news spread fast.

In all the noise and celebrating, though, I felt a
little overwhelmed. With all the hustle and bustle
surrounding Zach's arrival, I hadn't had much time to
myself—time which I needed after my encounters

with Zynthia and the hike up Courage Mountain. So two days after Zach had gotten well, I took a walk up to one of my favorite places in Vitreusia—the incline which overlooks the valley where the main village is located.

I sat down upon the soft grass with a relieved sigh. It was good to have a moment to myself. I began to sort through the memories of the quest, which were scattered in an awful sort of disarray in my brain.

My thoughts were interrupted by a familiar voice. "I must admit, the view from here is quite beautiful."

I whipped my head around to see who had spoken. I recognized the olive-skinned, black-haired girl at once and swallowed. "Zynthia?" I stammered out in utter surprise. "What—why—*how are you here?*"

She plucked at her bow. "My powers strengthen with each passing day."

"That's impossible! Vitreusia has been sealed from the Noxans!"

She smiled, a small, uncertain smile. "I guess not," she said quietly. A few moments of silence passed before she spoke up again. "It comes, you know," she said. "The war."

I just about choked on the air I was breathing. "What war?"

Her eyes turned to a cloudy shade of grey. "I will probably endanger myself by telling you this. I will attack Vitreusia with my army when I can split the barriers wide enough for us to get through."

"Lucem," I murmured, and a sphere of light appeared in my hand. "You would dare attack a

nation which has never done you any harm?!'"

"Thousands of Noxans have fallen by the hands of Vitreusians," she replied without making eye contact.

"We were defending ourselves!"

Zynthia threw up her hands. "What use is it to argue? The plan has been approved, and it will be carried out."

"I will not let you wipe out my entire race!" I cried.

"And I will not stand idly by while my nation crumbles at its very foundation!" she shouted back, her eyes changing to orange, and then back to grey. She sat down on a boulder, a tear creeping down her cheek. "I wish…we didn't have to be enemies…if only…Zenith…" Her voice cracked, and she did not make any attempt to continue speaking.

"Zynthia," I said, "we don't have to be enemies. We can work this out. Both our nations can exist— and exist in peace."

She shook her head. "No."

"Wha—"

She interrupted me. "Darkness and light cannot coexist, any more than day and night can be one and the same thing! Don't you understand? We are on opposing sides—which will soon clash. One will win. The other shall vanish. I would have liked to have a choice.." again her voice gave out, "but I don't. I can warn you. I can do nothing else." She stood up and began to veil herself in darkness.

"Zynthia, wait!" I called. To my surprise, she stopped. "Please, reconsider this. War…war is dreadful."

I could see her eyes turn to grey once more through the inky mist. "I know, Zach. I know."

She created a hole of blackness and stepped through it, and was gone. I ran my hand through my hair.

"Now what?" I thought to myself. This encounter could not be kept a secret. If I did *that*, the lives of all my countrymen would be at risk. I needed to tell someone…but then…did I have to tell them—any of them—right now? In the midst of my namesake's return and all the happiness? After all, Zynthia *had* said she wasn't yet powerful enough to break the barriers for a whole *army* of Noxans. The news could wait, I decided. For now, my world was safe.

♦ ♦ ♦

Leigh Hollis

When my brother's namesake miraculously recovered, it was determined by my mom, dad, and several others (all of whom were good friends of Aunt Leigh and Zach) that there should be a banquet to celebrate Zach's return. They planned it with very short notice, and I became extremely busy for a couple of days, helping with planning, cleaning, setting tables, all that stuff.

During my work I kept on wondering what else was in that ancient book which Zach and I had discovered just over two weeks ago.

I also speculated when it could have been

written. Such a book was easily a few millennium old, judging by the fancy calligraphy. Then there were the illustrations, which animated themselves as you looked upon them. How were they formed?

Late that night, while the rest of my family slumbered peacefully, I decided to sneak another quick look at the mystifying book. I tiptoed down the hallway and crept into our guest room, or "random room" as Zach and I had dubbed it.

The tome set upon the nightstand, glowing faintly. I picked it up and opened it gingerly, as if it were an explosive device that might go off if not handled carefully. The pages flew past, blown by the substantial breeze which came through the open window.

Then the wind abated, and I found myself looking at one of the last pages. It said:

There will come a day when a powerful darkness will arise, threatening to blacken Vitreusia's blue skies.

Vitreusian heroes, four, will unite, with the Sylvanians to fight the potent night; Vitreusia's most recent salvator, skilled in the ways of both peace and war, an inter duos, able to control the skies with a whim of his mind, Vitreusian twins, able to commune with one another through a single glance—and equally powerful in the ways of light.

They shall join the leader of the Sylvanians, a man trying hard to do what is best for his country. A great battle will ensue, with much loss on both sides, but in the end, the light will win, and the darkness shall subside.

I read it over again. *"This can't be about us—about me,"* I thought to myself. *"Zach can't control the skies—*

can he?"

No. My brother's namesake, although an inter duos, certainly could not manipulate the stars. Such an idea was preposterous. Some lunatic had gotten his hands on this book and written this rubbish on the second or third-to-last page.

I took deep breaths to calm myself down. It wasn't real. Perhaps surprisingly accurate in some ways, but not real. I closed the book and set it down on the nightstand, tiptoeing back to my room. I shouldn't have taken another peek. That so-called prophecy would haunt me for a long time.

Not wishing to share my unrest, I decided not to tell anyone about it—not even Zach. It was all the ravings of some madcap person anyway.

XV.

Leigh Kline

"Do I look okay?" I asked Zach when he emerged from his room. He swept over me with his hazel eyes.

"Okay is hardly the word for it, Leigh," he said.

"Oh, stop," I replied, warmth creeping into my cheeks. "Are you sure you're feeling okay?" I inquired of him. "If you don't feel well, you don't have to go. I'll stay home with you."

He laughed. "Leigh, I'm fine. I feel great..thanks to you."

"I couldn't have done it without you," I answered.

"I didn't do much of anything."

"Just freaked out your namesake completely…" I responded with a smile.

"I knew he could handle it."

"He's stronger than I ever thought…he and

Leigh both," I replied thoughtfully.

"They're destined for great things, those two," Zach said. "I can feel it."

"I think you're right," I said.

Then he took my hand. "I also feel that the two of us are destined to have a great night tonight," he said, smiling warmly. "Shall we go now?"

"I'm ready if you are."

We walked to the large house (dubbed the "festivity manor" by all the Vitreusians), which was decorated from pillar to roof, inside and out.

Zach shook his head in amazement. "It looks fantastic. And to think they spent only two days preparing everything!"

"I think we are well-liked," I mused.

Zach chuckled. "I don't know how I got mixed up in this—you're the one who saved this world singlehandedly."

I rolled my eyes. "That's not true. I had lots of help-a good deal of it coming from you."

"Don't give me *too* much credit, Salvator," Zach said with a wink.

"You're impossible," I said laughingly as we walked through the door.

Music was playing, and the large room (I'll just call it a ballroom) was chock full of Vitreusians, who were talking amongst themselves. As Zach closed the large, white door behind us, silence swept over the room.

A cheer arose from the multitude. Zach and I shook over one hundred hands before making it over to where Austin, Christina, and the twins sat. Austin stood up, and he and Zach shook hands and hugged. Christina hugged me first, then Zach, tears of happiness filling up her purple eyes.

We both greeted the twins and talked with them for a little while. I noticed Leigh fidgeting with a bracelet, which changed colors as she moved it about her wrist. *"Where did she get that?"* I wondered. *"I didn't see it on the expedition…"*

That thought exited my mind quickly, for I had two special people for Zach to meet.

"Come this way," I told him, and we began to weave through the crowd.

At last I found the couple I was searching for. The woman had straight, light brown hair and green eyes. The man had bright yellow hair and hazel eyes.

"Zach," I said, "I want you to meet Elisa and Lawrence. Elisa, Lawrence, this is your son, Zach."

Zach's hazel eyes, replicas of his father's, opened wide. Elisa's emerald green eyes began to tear up, and she embraced Zach tightly.

"I thought we'd never see you again," she sobbed.

Lawrence hugged both of them, mouthing two words to me. *Thank you.*

Elisa let go of Zach and gave me a hug as well. "Thank you, Leigh, honey," she said, tears flowing from her eyes.

"You're very welcome, Elisa," I replied. "I'm just as happy to have him back as you are."

Lawrence shook my hand heartily. "I echo my

wife's gratitude," he said. "All these years, that fateful night he was born has haunted us."

Elisa closed her eyes tightly. "I can still remember."

"As can I," Lawrence said. "I am glad that I have seen at last the splendid young man our son has become."

"Thanks, Dad," Zach said. "I…I do my best."

I left the three of them and went over to where Leigh stood alone, a pensive look on her face. She twisted her bracelet around and around her wrist, and she was so deep in thought that when I greeted her, she looked up with a start.

"Oh, it's you Aunt Leigh," she said. "Where's Zach?"

"Your brother?"

"No, your…friend."

"He's somewhere over there," I said, motioning with my right hand. "I introduced him to his parents."

Leigh's eyes widened. "Whoa. So he was living among them in Vitreusia and he didn't know it?"

"Yes," I replied. "Such a small world, isn't it?"

"I don't get it.."

I clapped my hand over my mouth. "Oh, dear. Even after all these years I still make Terran references."

Leigh laughed. "Well, I can't blame you—it's in your blood."

"I guess so."

"Speaking of which," Leigh said, casting a glance

in Zach's direction, "what exactly is in Zach's blood? I mean, he managed to stay half alive for years! Without any food or water or anything!"

I pursed my lips. "Well, Leigh, we may never find out. Zach's case is such a rare one. At this point, I'm just glad he made it. I'm content with that even if I never find out how or why he was able to do so."

"I'm so glad he's alright now," Leigh said. "I really like him already. Zach is already looking up to him, I can tell."

"That's great!" I said.

"Yep," she answered, nodding and twisting her bracelet, reminding me of a question I had been waiting to ask her.

"Leigh?"

"Yeah?"

"Where'd you get that bracelet?"

"Oh, that…" Was it just me or did her cheeks start to turn red? "…um, Tahigwa gave it to me. Before I left Sylvania."

"That was nice of him," I remarked.

"What do you think of him, Aunt Leigh?" Leigh asked abruptly.

"I think I know what's going on here.." I thought to myself.

Aloud I said, "Well, Leigh, I really didn't like him at first, but after I heard his story and after he helped us so much…I think very highly of him. He strikes me as a natural leader and someone who will do what he thinks is right for his country."

"That story of his was so sad.." Leigh whispered.

"It scares me that those fiends are still out there."

I swallowed. The thought made me nervous, too. "Tahigwa and his people are quite powerful. They can defend themselves, and if the Noxans launch a large-scale attack or something, we'll be right there to assist them."

"Vitreusia is still sealed from the Republic of Noxa, right?"

"Yes," I said, taking comfort in the answer.

Leigh sighed in relief.

Just then Zach came up behind me. "I hope I'm not interrupting anything," he said.

"Oh, no, we were just talking," Leigh answered.

"You're fine," I said, beaming at him.

"Good. May I talk to you outside, Leigh?"

I looked over at Leigh. "Which one?" I asked with a laugh.

"The one I stunt-drove for."

I laughed again. "Oh, okay then. See you later, Leigh."

Leigh waved goodbye and went back to fiddling with her bracelet.

Zach led me outside. It was a clear, cool night, with a gentle breeze that gave me goose-bumps. "This way," he said, weaving away from the village.

"Where are we going?" I queried.

"You'll see."

At last, he slowed to a stop. We were on top of a hill. "Leigh," he said, with an almost nervous undertone.

"Yes?"

"I want you...to hold out your hand and look up at the sky."

I did as he asked, bewilderment pervading every corner of my brain. I looked up and saw the Vitreusian constellations, nothing more.

Suddenly, I noticed something moving in the sky. A message began to write itself in stardust, glittering, a display of utter brilliance. I read the celestial note and gasped. *Leigh, will you marry me?* It said. I felt something cold in my hand. I looked down and saw a gorgeous silver ring. The jewel was square and a familiar shade of blue.

After wondering where I'd seen that color before for a moment or two, the answer came to me: *the sap*. I contemplated how this had been done, and Zach answered my unspoken question. "The jewelers of Vitreusia are quite talented," he said. "Once I explained my reason for wanting a drop of that sap, Christina was more than willing to get some from that vial."

I slipped the ring onto my finger. It was a perfect fit.

"Well, Zach," I said, "I'm...stunned. but I've also got an answer to your question."

I looked him in his hazel eyes and, grabbing his hand, helped him to his feet. "Yes."

Zach threw his arms around me tightly. For awhile we simply held each other. Zach sighed, a sigh that conveyed both relief and bliss.

Bending down (he was over half a foot taller than me), he gave me a gentle kiss on the cheek. "Leigh," he said, "I can't promise you that we will live 'happily ever after.'"

"That's okay, Zach," I breathed, concentrating on the steady sound of his heartbeat.

"However…"and here he smiled down at me in a lighthearted sort of way, "I *can* promise you the adventure of a lifetime."

I smiled, a smile bigger and more radiant than any smile that had ever crossed my face. "An adventure sounds wonderful," I said.

Zach's eyes twinkled like the stars in the sky. "Let's begin, then," he said. "Race you back!"

He started to sprint for the manor, and I followed him, unable to stop laughing, finding it impossible to cease smiling.

Later that night, after the news of our engagement had been broken, he toasted me. "To Leigh," he said, "my lifesaver, fellow adventurer, best friend, and fiancée. Here's to a journey like no other, which begins today and won't end for a long, long time."

Cheers filled the air, and I beamed at Zach and stood up. "To Zach, my stunt-driver, lifesaver, best friend, partner in every exploit, and fiancé. Here's to my most cherished story, one which begins years ago and hasn't been completed yet, nor will it be finished for years to come—the story of our relationship."

As the Vitreusians cheered, I stole a glance at Christina, Austin, and the twins. Christina's eyes were packed with tears of joy. Austin smiled broadly. Zach and Leigh were immersed in a silent yet playful argument, their purple eyes flashing messages to each other.

I turned back to Zach, and, rising up upon my toes, kissed him on the cheek. He tousled my hair, and I felt full inside. Full of joy, relief, courage. Joy that he was finally back next to me. Relief that the years of distress were over. And courage. Enough courage to last through whatever escapades had yet to come.

THE MIRROR

The adventures of Leigh and her friends are far from over. Here's a sneak peek at the next book in the Worlds Collide series:

The ShadowMaster

**SHE SHOULDN'T HAVE BEEN SCARED, STANDING
BEFORE THE REPRESENTATIVES IN THAT DARK,
TRIANGULAR ROOM.** She was young, tall, and
strong. They were aging, small, and of nominal
physical strength. The dark did not bother her—she
was a Noxan. Her very being was darkness.

No, it was the men themselves and their
intentions which made her olive-skinned hands
tremble and beads of sweat form on her forehead.

"You have been too lenient with them," one of
them said.

"I beg to differ, Xio," the girl answered, her
voice trembling. "We are not ready. My powers are
not sufficient to break the barriers. If I had killed or
wounded any one of their party, it would mean war."

Another one of the three spoke up. "Do you
mean to say that you would rather this war start later
than sooner?" he challenged.

"Silence, Yaotl!" said the third man. "Let her speak."

"Ah, so Zhubin has joined the coward's club," Yaotl taunted.

"I *will* have silence!" the girl shouted, summoning a black ball of mist into her hand.

"Yes, Zynthia," They all said together.

"Thank you," Zynthia returned coldly, barely managing to conceal the tremors in her voice. "It has just now become possible for me to break the barriers of Vitreusia, and for *me alone*. It will be some time before I am powerful enough to blast open the barrier for our army. Until then, I will scout. Keep the Sylvanians guessing."

"And the Vitreusians?" Xio inquired.

"I will leave them be."

"Leave them be?" Yaotl scoffed. "Leave them be? You can break through their barriers undetected. They, who have unmercifully slaughtered our kind! You can rip them apart from the inside out; destroy their world without any of them being able to explain what is happening. You can pervade their streets with terror and their homes with distrust. And yet…you do not."

Zynthia's eyes changed to a bright orange. "I am not like you, Yaotl. You should be glad of that, for not only would many Vitreusians lose their lives, but you would also be among the slain."

Yaotl's eyes changed to orange, and he sprung from his chair. "You," he sputtered, "are nothing more than an impudent child, and I curse the day I set eyes upon you and your brother Zenith."

At the mention of that name, Zynthia's eyes blazed a bright purple, and she unleashed a noose of mist, tightening it around Yaotl's neck. "Do not mention his name!"

Xio and Zhubin leapt from their chairs and rushed towards her.

"Stop!" Xio shouted.

Zynthia pushed them both into their seats with a wave of her hand. "Do not interfere. This is between the two of us." Then, turning back to Yaotl, "Never speak that name again," she said murderously, "if you do, it will be the last word that leaves your foul lips."

Yaotl, his eyes bugging out of his head, nodded, and Zynthia released her grip. The color vanished from her eyes as she looked around the room. "The same goes for the rest of you."

They all stood, ready to leave. "Zynthia.." said Zhubin.

"What is it?" she snapped.

"Brawls are breaking out as we speak. The casualties are extensive. We do not have much longer."

"Tell me something I do not know," Zynthia answered quietly. All three were silent. "Well?" she demanded. "If you have nothing to say, then leave me."

"Zy—" Zhubin began, but he was interrupted.

"*Leave me!*" They bowed and hurried out of the room, closing the door behind them.

As the sound of the door closing echoed off the

black walls, Zynthia Avariss fell to her knees, sobbing
brokenheartedly.

THE MIRROR

ABOUT THE AUTHOR

H. R. Kasper lives in Ohio on ten acres of land with her family, two dogs, and two affectionate outdoor cats. When not writing, she can be found photographing around her ten acres or playing some pickup basketball. Years and years ago, she too stretched out her hand towards her bedroom mirror…wondering if there really *might* be something besides her reflection on the other side.

Contact the author:

Twitter:@LuxVincemus
Email:hrkasperbooks@gmail.com

Made in the USA
Lexington, KY
14 November 2016